Bonfiggy Publishing
PO Box 119 Redmond,
Oregon 97756

First edition, 2025. Lucky you.
Cover, typesetting, and all other design: Lisa Dorn

Orders, inquiries, and pronouncements best accomplished
through joelbyronbarker.com

ISBN: 979-8-9938463-0-9

LCCN: 2025923622

FIC019000 FICTION / Literary
FIC080000 FICTION / Multiple Timelines
FIC040000 FICTION / Alternative History

CLEAR & SANE:

The Craft of The Green Paintbrush

A Novel

by Joel Byron Barker

TABLE *of* CONTENTS

the Green
Paintbrush

ABOUT THE AUTHOR

Joel Byron Barker fly fishes and runs and adores dogs. He has lived 96% of his life in Oregon, currently residing in the Central Oregon high desert. Along with Leo Marcel Schuman, he publishes about America's urban rural interchanges at oldtruckgoodcoffee.com.

The best job Joel ever had was pulling cable for computers and phones in 1997. He spent his off time writing long poems to try to sort the world out. To this day he is seeking ways to braid together community, technology, and the outright unstoppable beauty around us.

DEDICATION

Dedicated to the real TSE, WCW, EP, & HD –
The ones who were blood-pumping beings,
not points of discussion.

1

CLEAR *and* SANE

[1982-83]

EVEN old Senator Kilby knew that it would be a new and challenging world for everyone.

For six months, the government purchased television spots, newspaper ads, and of course billboards to promote the date. If for some reason a driver had not heard about the court battle or the Senate battle before that on the Clear and Sane Roads bill – promptly shortened to CSR by pundits and headline writers – then they would most certainly have been unable to miss the largest concerted advertising campaign up to that time. Kilby wanted to give everyone a fair chance – and no excuses.

To the pundits and speech writers, CSR was born out of exhaustion with the world as it was. A world where we spoke of fidelity but thought only of promiscuity. Where we claimed fealty but acted only in our own interest. Where laws were threatened but never enforced. The message resonated deep in the hearts of America's Mothers, America's Law Enforcement Industry, and America's Disenfranchised Old People.

CSR was not without controversy, but its supporters were many. Its supporters were true believers. Its supporters were vocal and accepted instruction well.

The good Senator from Delaware was an old man, but not ignorant to the changes in the world. He was surprisingly spry when it came to technology. He had a computer at home, an Apple II, which he used for writing speeches as well as a reported obsession with Oregon Trail. He often compared his Oregon Trail games with his younger staffers. They in turn played more Oregon Trail so that they would have material for chats with "The Old Dysentery."

It was just lucky chance for Carl Stoner that Kilby was in the Oregon Trail headspace. Carl just needed a senator, deeply entrenched, who wanted one last great bill.

Carl, a 6'5" ghost of a man, was as gentlemanly as anyone could expect from a man raised in the mid-upper crust of Los Angeles. He had spent his first few years in DC living well outside the beltway and had learned a great deal about the South from this Southern town. He gave respect until people demonstrated that they did not deserve it.

Carl's client was the second largest insurance provider (as calculated by dollar value of all contracts) in the United States. They wanted to be the first largest provider. They hired Carl to help get them there.

Within the headquarters of the second largest insurance provider in the US, an executive vice president was trying to think of how to impress the board that he had what it took to be the next chief executive (often termed the CEO). The current CEO was showing signs of age, but had not done anything drastically wrong. If he was replaced in a situation that was not traumatic, it was possible that the board would select someone from within the organization instead of going to a heroic CEO from the outside.

One year ago in 1982, this senior VP (named Don) was walking small circles around the elevator on the way to his office. "I could make us number one." He thought. The elevator opened and he walked towards his office. "Is there any way to overcome the market leader?" Don had an MBA and recalled in a class once talking about how market leaders are made. Established market leaders rarely lost their lead without some change in the rule book.

He decided to change the rule book. "All we need is a disruption in the insurance market and we will be ahead of them."

What needs to change? Cars themselves? Roads? Rules of the Road! If they could change the rules of the road, they could eliminate their competitor's competitive advantage. If we wrote the bill, we can claim those customers before anyone knows.

So Don created this idea all on his own. He proffered it to the board one sunny day in their traditional quarterly meeting room, a windowless office appointed in the latest contemporary office style for '82. All the men of the board sat together, thirteen suited fellows at a table, smiling and laughing. They liked to be in each other's company and each enjoyed the moment when the other twelve turned and quieted down to listen to him alone.

Don had asked to make a presentation, updating the board on growth strategies in Personal Insurance. Behind a couple of pie graphs on his flip chart, he had a page that simply read "Legislative Agenda, 1983."

At the and of the presentation, all thirteen men felt it necessary to say at least one thing, whether it was a question built around a special word or a sentence that started with, "In my experience..." Don had achieved agreement for his plan. The stenographer was directed to restate the conversation simply as "Corporation management updated the board on the ongoing legislative agenda."

Don had needed to speak with Carl prior to the presentation. The two had met for lunch one afternoon at an Arctic Circle Restaurant near to the The Second Largest Insurance Company in America's Corporate Headquarters. Carl was in Salt Lake City because The United States Congress was in recess while the members returned to their states to campaign. It was early fall, 1982.

Carl took that as an opportunity to travel about and visit his clients. He had scheduled three days in Salt Lake City to make a presentation for the senior leadership and then make himself available for hushed lunches such as this. The two sat on colorful plastic chairs outside the restaurant. Carl had a burger in front of him. Don had a halibut sandwich.

"It could be done." Carl said, "We would use the safety angle, I think. Get moms with injured children. Follow them with some white coated researcher types to show how we can make sure that there are no more Mrs. Frafanoogle's who lose their daughters too young."

Excitement built up in the back of Don's throat. This was all so interesting and new to him, but he felt that he could be really good at it. "I was thinking about it as an offering to the sanity of America."

Carl briefly forgot himself and took an open-mouthed chew. He swallowed while Don actively paused and stared, his eyes a pathway straight into the curious sense of purity and excitement that Don had found while talking to Carl. Carl glanced over Don's shoulder at the giant colorful chicken behind Don that contained the speaker and microphone of the drive-through.

Carl thought that Don and the chicken briefly had the same expression about the eyes. Don followed Carl's gaze self-consciously. It was a relief to Carl that Don's eye-popping subsided when his concentration broke.

"The sanity of America. I guess I am not seeing it." Carl stopped himself from saying any more by putting the burger back into his mouth.

"Yes, look. A young boy in the back seat, watching his dad drive. He is, say 10 years old and emulates his father whenever he can, so he watches dad carefully. Here he is, driving. Someday, the boy thinks, I will drive – like my father, right? He looks at the speedometer, then he looks at a sign they pass. Speed limit 80 km/h. He looks back at the dashboard. Speed, 100. 'Dad! You're going too fast!' His dad is breaking a rule! Oh no! But Dad says 'Its alright son, everyone does it.' So, the boy thinks, we don't follow rules and everyone KNOWS that we don't follow rules, but the rules are still there. Is that true of all rules? How do I know which rules to follow? It drives us all just a little bit crazy. Don't you see, Carl? Everybody thinks about this but nobody says anything because nobody else is saying anything so we all think that it is only us, that we are alone in feeling that THIS WORLD MAKES NO SENSE."

Don crushes a fry repeatedly against his tray to emphasize every word. Carl briefly wonders if Don is emphasizing each word – each container of meaning – or each syllable – each musical, metrical unit. He consciously adjusts his facial expression and glances only briefly at the chicken, then back to Don.

"Everyone is thinking 'either the whole world is insane, or I am insane.' Everyone pushes this thought away every day, they brush their teeth and get on with it. But here, this unresolved nugget remains. When is a rule a rule? When is it a giant convenient lie? We can offer clarity, a clear and fair understanding to people. We can offer them peace, a quiet mind where once there was confusion, cacophony."

Carl was glad that he had a fry in his mouth when Don paused so that he could chew for a second and collect himself. It allowed him to prevent the first couple of possible replies.

"I would never have thought of that, Don."

With Carl's advice, Don was able to put together his presentation for the board. With the board's vote-less say so, Don was able to go back to Carl and give him the green light. Don went to work preparing a plan that would position The Second Largest Insurance Company In America for the new face of American driving. Carl had told him that it would take at least one year, maybe two, before the law would pass.

Occasionally, over the next couple of months, Don would send Carl "some ideas he had" about how to position the bill as an issue of American Mental Health. He capitalized American Mental Health. Carl could tell, even though Don's handwriting was somewhat inconsistent, the A, M, and H were clearly magnified.

So Carl found Senator Kilby, Senator Kilby found a reason to take on the project. His staff found a hapless little Delaware state organization of victims of car accidents. Off to the races went the new bill, a policy-forming glob of funding, enforcement directives, and penalties that made it a very bad idea to speed at all, anywhere.

Kilby, with his interest in technology, actually contributed the germ of the technology solutions that really sexed up the bill. With a dab of budget-neutral R&D fund redirection, they were able to get speeders photographed and ticketed automatically from roadsides. The team was fortunate to discover that a German company was already making a device that can do this. In a flurry of America-first enthusiasm they redirected grant money specified for helping America Stay Competitive.

Carl was pretty proud of his work. He managed to wrangle all the different parties and get the right words in the right mouths – all without getting his name or The Second Largest Insurance Company In America attached too prominently to any mainstream press about the movement.

A big project like this is never without its snags. His initial head counts in the Senate were a little off and it looked like they were going to have to back down from some of the provisions to get the bill through. In a play to get those last few votes, he reached into the back of a drawer and pulled out one of Don's hand written American Mental Health letters. He put it next to his Rolodex and flipped through to John Palto. John was the lobbyist for a very large alliance of people concerned about mental health issues. He also lobbied for some mine operators in Nevada and an association of infant clothing manufacturers.

John had the ear of a couple congressmen and he famously could bring in constituents who were compelling and a little discomfiting without being overtly dangerous. Some monies were allocated to targeted counseling programs for motor vehicle aggression and John delivered a couple more congressional votes.

The press picked up on Don's language, ably injected by Carl, about a nationwide emotional trauma caused by inconsistently applied rules. It got a whole lot more traction than Carl expected.

So, almost a year after the first Arctic Circle meeting, in early Fall of 1983, America woke up, got in their cars, and tried very very hard to not speed ever again.

The roads were covered in new police in vehicles specifically designed for the traffic stop. Some were visible, but scofflaws and the inattentive quickly learned that a road with no traffic authorities visible was surely under the eyes of an invisible aggressor. Either a robot that simply photographed you quietly and mailed you a very expensive bill or a hidden motorcyclist.

A great deal of innovation in enforcement happened in the next year. Precincts with a new directive and new federal dollars – to say nothing of the promise of their share of fines – tried a variety of approaches and proudly shared their successes with their brothers in other locales. Soon police were taking impounded beaters and turning them in to low-profile cruisers, at the ready to turn on their lights and pull over unsuspecting speeders.

Certainly that first year of Clear And Sane Roads was not good for American Mental Health in general.

It was good for Don and for The Second Largest Insurance Company in America, which can no longer be called by that name.

Even as Carl was padding about the halls of Congress having quiet discussions, Don had set out to prepare his company for the change.

Don had not exactly worked himself to Senior Vice President from the ground up, but had done some time as a mid-level manager in different departments. He thrived in these positions. When meeting with his superiors he would be silent as they offered their leadership insights, turning on a reassuring, congenial manner transmitted mostly through body language and facial tics that said, "I am quite awkward, but please don't take it personally. No really; be comfortable." Don had been branded Management Material, and then Upper Management Material.

For three years, Don headed up a small team of actuaries, a sort of skunk works team for The Second Largest Insurance Company in America. The hand-picked corps of number wizards took creative approaches to statistical problems. If The Second Largest Insurance Company in America considered offering pet insurance, the problem was put to Don's team. Should a corporate client's product start strangling babies, it might come to Don's team to determine the value of the client down the road – including the probability the company would be forced into bankruptcy from a liability law suit – to help the account team decide how cooperative and forthcoming to be. They were called the Strategic Actuarial Department. All members had signed agreements to not speak about their work to anyone except their spouse. Their spouses had signed similar agreements.

Don knew that he would not have much access to the Strategic Actuarial Department (SAD) while working on Sane Roads. In 1982, when a mysterious disease began killing gay men in San Francisco, the SAD was asked to seek opportunities within the numbers. Don did not need the entire SAD team, however.

He did not go straight to his own office when he left his Arctic Circle lunch with Carl.

There was a spacious, windowed room down the hall from Don's office. The door read **Cardio Plathemy Senior Account Advisor**. If you knocked and then opened the door, Cardio was usually standing up. If he had his hands out of his pockets, his fingers were splayed tents on a circular glass topped table (with silver accents) that took up the bulk of the room. His back bent slightly but engaged as a sprinter waiting, waiting for the starting gun.

Don knocked, waited for the slight, muttered yelp, then opened the door.

Cardio might have his back to the door or he might be facing the door. It gave Don the impression that Cardio orbited that table like a slow moon.

That day, Cardio wore a tight vest over his tapered midriff, matched to his pants. The grey flannel went well with the pink pinstriped shirt. He moved his eyes more than his head when Don came through the door. He turned back to the collection of papers – many colors and sizes, arrayed in an apparent system across the face of the glass table – in front of him, took a pencil up in his right hand while his left steadied a creamy page of European A4 dimensions and made a small line at the end of a hand-drawn table.

"Don."

"Card." Cardio smiled as usual at the unwanted shortening of his name. Don turned and shut the door. His left hand on the handle and his right fingers pushing the door about two feet above the handle to assure a quiet but complete latching. Then he turned to his own personal math wiz and explained that he needed to know how to survive in the insurance business when the world turned upside down.

Cardio has an exotic face, which he is aware of. Cardio thinks more than other people, which he is aware of. Cardio is aware, but does not tell other people, that he sometimes formulates sentences in his head but realizes that they are only numbers and functions strung together. He then has to translate that thought into a language that other people can understand. Incidentally, he speaks three languages, two fluently and one functionally. Don speaks one.

"So, you are setting this in motion but you don't know how our company will benefit yet?"

"Yes. We will have a head start. And, we have you."

"Our competitors, they have actuaries and analysts, too."

"But they don't have you. What are you working on now?"

Cardio lowered one eyebrow and explained his current project as "parsing a few tawdry differentials." He said that he could have it done by next Wednesday and would start on the remapping of car insurance Thursday.

2

AT *the* SHOW

[2003]

CARDIO is not the only person of his age in this venue. He is tall enough that he has scanned the crowd and noticed the obvious over 40s. Most are men. A lot are alone. An equal number of them linger in the back, squeeze in mid-pack, and have shouldered themselves to the front.

He had bought the ticket far in advance. The popular Spokane club booked her for a week night, not a weekend show favored to sell out, but he did not know that and wanted to make sure he had access to the experience.

Mary's album had found him like an arrow. His careful scans of culture had picked it up, snagging his attention by the corner when a critic got caught up misusing his memory of The Bible to contort Mary's album "Delilah" into an anti-religious satire. The article pulled in extensive lyric quotes, and they stuck into Cardio's mind as the relevance of the article quickly faded into deep storage.

The confounding, the contorting of the author slowed Cardio down. He stepped out of the office one day, found his way to the record store, and bought the album.

He did not start reading voraciously about Mary until he had spent that first night alone with her. He started cooking a dinner for one, put the CD into his stereo.

"Matter, what's the matter."

He looked up, nodded, then returned to chopping a single carrot.

He chops a half an onion. The scent is perfect for the music. It calls to you, it hurts you, and you manage to stand still and let it wash over you. You want to stand still and feel the moment, be overpowered and see the end of that invisible force.

He listened a second time, after finishing his dinner. He opened the CD case, took out the book, and read the simply-printed lyrics. He took a pen and marked up the page, drawing arrows across the lines to make clear how the third track remembers the first and alludes to the seventh.

Then Cardio started reading about Mary. He picked up the music fan magazines, the industry magazines that focus on market segments and genre trends. There were three literary writers who built mention of Mary. He found them all. He set up a tool to query web crawlers for mentions of "Mary" and "Delilah." It allowed him to find these points that she had woven together, the mention in Time Magazine, the photographic associations with celebrities in People, and the Rolling Stone extended interview.

He could see into it, looking askance at her and what trailed behind her. The grooves in the sand that her heavy cloaks made.

And she challenged the more daring writers. Their weak interpretations, like the first article he found, caused him to love her, and to feel unnaturally close to her even though they never met. She did not know of Cardio, but he felt a kinship. That if they had a few minutes together they would become dear friends, laughing, offering lights for each other's cigarettes, prodding fun that can only be built on the deepest understanding of how the other is put together.

He bought that ticket long before the show. He went through a lot of scenarios to imagine what it would be like. It was unlikely that they would meet, no matter how beautiful that meeting would be for both of them.

He's here now, in a sea of young faces. He's holding a drink, a double Basil Hayden whiskey with no ice in a narrow glass he had to point at. The bartender thought it was ridiculous but found himself too busy to even express that this was confusing. He poured the drink. Cardio paid cash and waited for his change.

The show started 40 minutes late, something he had not foreseen.

"Matter, what's the matter?"

Cardio lowers the glass to his hip. His fingers tip it upright as the angle of it moves past where his wrist could keep it level. He is holding on to the rim and the glass dangles at his thigh. He tips his chin up a little bit. His eyebrows are at attention.

It's an amazing feeling, to be above them all like that. Two songs in and she is washing over him.

There is not a good measure of sincerity, but he is watching her dispense it in mighty portions.

After the second song it is time for some chit chat. She tweaks her guitar, her capo, she taps foot pedals.

"Spokane, Spokane, Spokane.

Seems like a nice town for experiments." She turns and makes brief eye contact with the multi-instrumentalist.

"No one talks about experiments that went right. Maybe tonight you will start one. Or maybe tomorrow in the sober light of day. That's a good time for experimenting, too. Here's a song about an experiment going well."

Cardio puts in his pocket the thought that experiments should be faced objectively, not with a desire for success or fear of failure. Experimenting is without any investment in one outcome or the other.

Mid-thought, Mary and her band blast the room back, blowing the audience away from them.

In small clubs like this, they can't get the lighting effect to sync with the music. The song relies on the zero-warning harmony+tone salad+beat extravaganza. Tonight, they crushed Cardio with the volume and the percussion patterns while a new voice and instrument threads all needed to be figured out all at once and then all started fading again.

The bassist watches every head in the room kick back or blink or smile in relief.

Cardio is uplifted, is surrendered. He stops figuring. He can't figure. There is not a measure for it. The sole of his right foot lifts up off the ground briefly. Toe last, then heel first back down.

The percussion settles in to something manageable. The bass player watches faces calm and start to bob together.

There is not a measure for it right now.

After the third song Cardio lights a cigarette. In a place like this you can simply flick your cigarette toward the floor. It's an amazing feeling.

Then it was over. There was a moment he was blank, and then a moment to walk through. The white house lights came on. Cardio walked toward the door. When he heard Mary sing, he thought everything had been worth it.

3

CARDIO *and* HIS REST

[2022]

CARDIO is sitting in a comfortable-looking cane chair at the end of a hallway. The door next to him is open and afternoon light from the window falls upon his feet. He has a cup of tea next to him on a heavy end table. It is more of a prop than a refreshment. The long-term residents are not fooled, but they do not care and he does not care if they care. He takes a disinterested sip of the tea.

He sees patterns, he always has. That essentially has been the job. As you progress, you release your ego and become less fragile. You work more easily. Then eventually you lose any sense of mastery and become forever the novice. The patterns are greater than you, but to be seen they need you. You have to breathe into them, mortalize them. By their nature, it is a simplification – a relief for these viewers (executive, tactical, or whatever), but you know them, the patterns. All the patterns, including the ones inside of the executives and the tacticians. They are not matter, they cannot be grasped. We create a simulacrum, a fake that can be printed out. Touched, pointed to. Most people need that. Patterns alone are not natural for people. Once you have given up trying for mastery you can be a novice for the rest of time, the rest of your time. Really befriend the patterns. Like when someone sits at the bar because there is a social emptiness in his heart. He calculates that bars are a good place to be. That if you are in a bar that the bar itself presents up to two places a new friend or lover could sit. The pattern: Someone sits down once. He has done this ten times with no result and the eleventh time you get a short conversation. No ongoing relationship. Our subject repeats the behavior. The 27th time he gets a similar result. The 60th time he meets someone that he has sex with shortly thereafter. Success of a sort. Mostly a sad inevitability, not fulfillment. Watch that, Reginald. Pattern? A flick of a coin in the air. All of us who think about it know that there are no patterns in flipped coins.

A train just passed the building. Some rushed to the windows.

Sorry, no. The flipped coin. There is no actual pattern, but we can sell ourselves and each other on patterns. But it is not an actual pattern. The pattern is from the breath of God, forming the present at every moment. Those in a quest for patterns want to own the future. They seek advantage. They want to rule. Patterns are the key to ruling. They tell you when the comet will appear, right? When the rains will come. We are things, not patterns. I am a thing. You are a thing. I can touch you. You are not a pattern. I have been asked for patterns. I have been asked for actionable information from watching the breath of God. To be honest, I loved it. I love it. My mind was fully engaged. I liked the problems. I provided salient answers. I still can act like a master for periods of time. Then, like an amateur, like a novice, I watch patterns helplessly. I tell the paying customers that maybe, that maybe they could justify some worry that at the end of the day, that please understand about patterns. But they don't want to. Patterns are hymns they want to sing. Singing a true pattern is like singing a baseball game. Don't believe in me. Don't believe in results. Definitely don't believe in these patterns. They don't repeat. The trends are well hidden in motifs that look like noise. Even those trends do not care about outcome. They don't win or lose. Reginald, I think I understand. I write him letters, I did so this morning. He reads them. I read his work and there is a pattern or two I recognize.

Some days Cardio has visitors.

4

REGINALD

[2010]

REGINALD woke up, again. That kept happening. Is it true for everyone else that the first act of waking is remembering?

No, it is the second act for most people. The first act of awakening is the question why. Only the obsessed and those too tired to fight anymore skip the question why and start in on remembering.

Reginald could not sleep anymore, and just folding and unfolding his body under the blankets was going to ruin him, with remembering.

He got up.

In the hallway he came across his bike. That was encouraging.

He took a piss with one eye closed, idly moving his hips to direct the stream around the toilet bowl. Lesser men used their fingers to aim their dick. Didn't flush the toilet. Save water.

For lack of anything better to do, he turned on the radio and prepared food. Some black beans from the fridge, an egg, and a corn tortilla. Reginald is allergic to wheat, a celiac.

This is a fucking great day to get outdoors. Highs in the low seventies, sun expected, no rain in the valley. It looks like Spring might be here early. Skip school.

He likes that those who have this condition are called celiac. The -iac ending suggests a medical description of something harsh and natural. Maniac. Celiac. Cardiac. Stand back! I think he is a celiac. (Crowd ooohs and quakes.)

These old sash windows freak him out a bit. It takes a good amount of force to get them moving. He can picture the window slamming up, then all the glass cracking down on to his exposed wrists. You actually have to do a little squat to get them going, lifting with a knee motion that you transfer through your back to your shoulders and then slide upwards with your arms.

Same concept as a jumpshot.

He got the window open. The air shifted around him. He leaned his head out to just beyond the border between inside and outside. He tilted his head slowly up, and then down. His nostrils flared. He had his back to his life and his eyes closed.

He had punched the screen out months ago.

Hack was jostling his shoulder from the passenger seat and saying "Reg, Reg, wake up." They had a question for him. Something pretty good. He does not want to lose that. What was the question?

On the off-chance that Kell was outside, Reginald opened his eyes. He could make out the path of the cool air from the greenery along the river, over the boulevard, and up to his window.

No one resembling Kell in the courtyard. For better or worse.

This is agonizing. What was the question? It had some sort of philosophical bent and yet it was clearly a time killing act for a long drive. Should it come to anything would be an outright miracle, but what a thing to do to get on down the road, less crazy.

Something religious maybe. Predestination? We can never figure out predestination, so that comes up. That is weird, isn't it? We all instinctively believe in predestination on one level, but we refuse to accept a theological basis for it. Is this a purely American quandary? I ask you.

But that is not what they asked. It was a really great question. Reg thought that he should call Hack and ask. Hack might remember. However, if he did not then he would offer a bunch of dumb dick-related questions as possible options.

Reginald was not feeling like parrying dick related questions just now. In fact, he was still tilting his head up and down slowly in the open air. His eyes have finished surveillance and closed again.

Possibly due to an accident five years ago, he cannot comfortably tilt his head up to where he believes that other people can. It starts to hurt and he slows and stops in the middle, at about the angle that one holds their head most of the time on most days. Unless you are hanging out with really tall people, perhaps. Or really short people. However it is harder to make fun of short people and not offend. Tall people are generally not touchy about it, short people might be midgets.

On the kitchen table, along with four unopened envelopes and a bowl of sea salt, was a set of keys and a heavy leather bag. Reginald put his open palm on the surface of the bag and gripped it slightly as he walked by. Still barefoot, still in the light cotton pants he likes to sleep in. Still the center of a silent whirlwind in an empty field. Wide open.

That question: it did wake him up that day and they talked about it for a while. How to get at that memory? Reginald decided a long time ago that different people's memories function differently. It is not something that he cataloged or documented at all, but he tried to use it to create profiles of the people that he met.

He thinks of his memory as ego-associative, that things are remembered in clusters related to his identity. As such, it is hard to recall something based on when it occurred. He can not string things together on timelines very well. Perhaps he just is not interested in doing so. Perhaps.

So he tosses around ideas with himself: Memories or other tidbits that might cluster with the philosophical question that woke him in the back of a speeding car.

Sunlight and sleep together.

Hack and Jess.

Being needed.

Self doubt, concealed.

Nothing worked. He should make lunch or shower, whichever feels more urgent or enjoyable.

We will figure out what the question was. This is the sort of thing that works out into something interesting.

Reginald has not checked his phone for messages in over fifteen minutes. He does so now. He hopes for something to respond to. Something to define this morning. There is nothing. No texts, no voicemail notifications. He is alone in the apartment.

And this question. You can't search the Internet for your own memory. It is not yet eight o'clock. Everyone who was in that car is not typically responsive to phone calls at this hour. A text would also fall on deaf ears. Maybe. Here. How about a text to all three of them like this:

You woke me in the back of a car to talk about a question. Heading into E. Oregon desert. What was the question?

He has a number for Hack. Phil as well. Not Jess, but she is probably in the same bed as Hack even now. Wow. So long those two have been together. Longer than that question. What if that question is what keeps them bonded? What if revealing that question would destroy their bond?

Reginald is alone in the house, but he makes a dramatic face. He stands next to the kitchen table and looks out the window, straight at the kitchen window of his neighbor. No one is there but some houseplants.

In his right hand he is gripping his cell phone. He fills his lungs with air and exhales loudly. His right arm brings the phone before his face. His left hand pushes and holds a button on the top of the device, along the chipped chrome surface. The phone glows at his face, sings a little tune, then goes dark. He turns and puts it on the table.

He takes the leather satchel up off the table and walks to the living room. He sits in a low-backed chair. Two hands flip open the top of the bag. He pulls out a plain soft cover booklet. He holds it in his hands. His right thumb bends back the entire book then rolls away from the pages, allowing each one to quickly click to view and then be subsumed by the next.

Reginald's thumb stopped when blank pages started appearing, then he flipped back to the first of them. A pen was clipped under the front flap of the satchel. He took that in his right hand.

He has not yet eaten or said anything aloud since he woke.

He writes for a while, pausing very little. Reginald's head gets closer to the page, sagging off his shoulders.

He has to turn the page to continue, having filled two facing panes.

He hates what he just wrote, but keeps going.

This is just awful. He can barely keep writing.

He has to stop. He sighs. The book goes onto an end table. He stands up from the chair and returns to the kitchen table. Reginald powers the phone back on. He stoops his head down and watches the entire boot process of the little computer.

He dials Hack, who Reginald is certain will not even hear the rings. When voicemail picks up, Reginald says, "Hack, three years ago you woke me when I was sleeping in the back of Jess's car out somewhere, on the way back from Boise that one time. Remember that time? Give me a call."

The sun is coming up, finally. The radio is still blabbering. An announcer is grafting curse words together:

"Fit." "Shuck." "Cunck."

Reginald makes coffee. There has not been a traffic report even though he has had the radio on for an hour. There are never any traffic reports any more.

Reginald is 25 years old. He lives in Spokane, Washington in a single story brick apartment complex built around a courtyard. He has lived here for 18 months. He is not sure why.

His appreciation of morning radio is new. He used to think the squawky, manipulative voices and the preference for chatter over music was undesirable. For the last three and a half months, Reginald has been listening carefully to the morning radio shows.

It is early fall, 2010. A peaceful morning. No news to report.

The leather bag goes over Reginald's shoulder and he pedals to his office. He is retracing his path from a few hours ago when he returned, drunk and exhausted, to home. He bikes by the corner where he came across that unfortunate army.

Downtown Spokane is old, tall buildings set on large blocks. It has a majesty about it, particularly when the streets are underpopulated. The looming buildings draw your attention. Reginald knows that he tends to personify them, and enjoyed watching himself do so as he made his way out of the bar, down the street back to his office where he had left his bike. It was late, the bartenders were about to turn on lights and hustle drinks away from the last enthusiasts.

On his way back toward the office, Reginald trailed a swaying mass of men, perhaps eight fellows, wrapped around a stumbling man that needed one person to keep him upright and in motion. His efforts were not helped by another friend – equally drunk but able to walk unaided – who slapped him on the back and pushed at his ribs.

Reginald was some distance behind the group, so he could not make out a lot of details. He could hear voices, a mix of urgency and thrill, of directives and expressives. And the people were so small under the buildings, so small that the buildings did not even bother to look down upon them, but rather the buildings listened and looked at each other. If their expression changed, it was imperceptible, only enough for the buildings to say, each to each, "I know."

These stone buildings blocked the sightlines of many street corners, and the group ahead had very little warning when they intersected the other drunken gaggle. Reginald closed on them as the two hydras took each other in.

It was startling, the parallels. A slightly smaller collection of women, similarly dressed, surrounding a woman in a tiara, an electric-green boa, and an oversized white t-shirt smudged with words. She was not doing a great job of standing still.

The core of the male group wore a similar shirt, and a hat which Reginald could not quite interpret except that it was embarrassing, perhaps two bare plastic breasts sprouting like Mickey Mouse ears. This moment was a unique and curious moment. A roving bachelor party encountered a roving bachelorette party on a street corner. At first Reginald considered that the two were betrothed, but determined through the confusion of the groups that they were in fact not engaged to be married to each other, had simply been brought out by their friends on the same night, ahead of two separate weddings, to drink heavily and perform a sort of scavenger hunt driven by the items printed on the shirts that they wore.

It was a funny moment, and an ugly one. Depending on the mood of the passerby, one of those judgments could be greater than the other. A taller woman, also wrapped in a tiara, nimbly dove into the male crowd and grabbed the bachelor's hand. He, a bit shorter, raised his head carefully to look at her as she started talking.

"Ok. Ok. Ok. So..."

Reginald skirted the crowd and crossed the street. He could not see the building's faces as he got on his bike, his thoughts with the bachelor collision, a colorful and disgusting cacophony. He biked home without further incident, as best he can recall.

The Green Paintbrush office is the fifth floor of one of those buildings that Reginald empathizes with. He wheels his bike into the elevator and hits the button. At the fifth floor he notices that his head feels very heavy and does not raise it when the door opens. The drivetrain ticks as he turns to the left from the elevator and pushes his bike to his corner of the large room.

Reginald has worked for The Green Paintbrush for two years and has never met Cardio.

5

REGINALD *meets* FORTH

[2031]

REGINALD himself, when looking at a timeline such as his own life, would say that to understand the river you should float downstream, eventually to the mouth of the river and to the sea, which will really explain everything. Looking upstream is looking at the still, silent, and dead.

Reginald faces the western window. The sky gives off gray light and presses into the room. To his right, he can see the edge of the front and a shocking blue. He cannot tell which direction the front is moving and does not predict if the weather will change, here.

"So Mr. Cashon, I would like you to meet Forth," Sean speaks loudly, as if he were on an international phone call in a crowded room.

Forth strides past Sean and extends his hand, long before he reaches Reginald. His whole body, moussed hair to buckle shoes, red cuff to silver metal suit buttons, is open, welcoming, enthusiastic.

"Thank you so much for meeting me, Mr. Cashon. It is such a pleasure for me to finally meet you."

Reginald stands, turns, and tugs down the back of his suit coat. He tries to get his own hand up in time to join Forth's advancing greeting.

"Forth, good to meet you as well."

Forth sits next to Reginald, without flourish. As much as he expected anything, he expected flourish. Sean does his best to be unassuming while taking pictures of the two famous men together, incongruously chatting in an otherwise empty room. Reginald had previously signed a form that gave permission for the inc. version of Forth's band to have control of these pictures "for promotional purposes."

"Thank you for the invite. I was very complimented by your letter."

"My minister is a great fan – a reader – of your work. He gave me Samson to read several years ago. I have followed you ever since. I appreciate the unvarnished way you talk of your faith in your recent work."

"Well thank you. I have never thought of it as unvarnished, although I do believe that poetry is no place for varnish of any kind. I take that as a high compliment."

Reginald pushes his shoulders back into the chair by gripping each chair arm and straightening his elbows.

"Touché. I suppose that is a difference in our work. A pop song needs to be just the right blend of grit and varnish. I put in something that people can relate to and something that lifts them up, something to transport them."

"Yes, I can see that. Seems that most songs have an implied didactic purpose. A poet's work should be reportorial."

"Primarily reportorial, right? Surely there is some instructiveness in something like Paradise Lost."

'Instructiveness' repeated a half a dozen times in Reginald's head. He blinked slowly.

"Not in the least. I must disagree. You can tell an instructive poem because it is a bad poem."

Forth was glancing around the room, but at this he looks quickly up to meet Reginald's eyes. Reginald had bent his elbows again but his back remains straight. A short silence ensues. Forth leans forward. His shoulders narrow. Layers of clothing rumple as he puts his elbows on his knees and clasps his hands.

"I don't understand. Can you explain?"

One of Reginald's hands swivels to his face as though he was wiping cobwebs away before him.

"My poems, I try to make them the best reportage I can manage, but I am not reporting on El Salvador or Dallas-Fort Worth International Airport. I am reporting from wherever I am. I do not report on subjects such as the effects of war on the third world or the breaking of a heart."

"But Samson – isn't that about the dissolution of knowledge by technology? '...and we lost all our fingertips to the keys...'"

Reginald continues to wait a long time before responding. Forth releases a quiet half cough.

"Well, I can see how that material stands out for you. Certainly several critics have called that out as well. I came across that issue of technology while finding a voice of a young man striving to express himself in polite society without coming off as a psychotic imbecile. Of a man who had been convinced that there was a cliff for culture, that the hordes were coming for us.

"Obviously, he had been misinformed of the hordes. No hordes as of yet," he looks over his shoulder out the window, as if the angry middle of America could be assaulting the foundation of this European high rise. He is glad to see it is not. Still relieved, still surprised, still disappointed that it never came.

Forth pauses this time.

"You."

"As such as me."

"And they call me egotistical."

"Perhaps ego, perhaps. I am not quite sure. My subjects, the subjects of all good poetry..."

"always good poetry."

"has a last known address somewhere in proximity to the poet's ego. Before I joined the church I found this source, this powerful upwelling, to be selfish and indulgent. To be honest I was sometimes caught in reveries on the selfishness of writing poetry, of writing at all."

Reginald is no longer slow and considered. He does not press against the chair. His legs are unfolded and his hands rest in his lap when they are not needed for sparse gesturing.

"Before you joined the church..."

"Yes, before I joined the church. And briefly after. In fact moreso. Why, I asked myself, was I occupying my life with these selfish works and not celebrating the kingdom of God?"

"To turn your talents towards exhorting The Lord on earth? That sounds as instructive as can be."

"Indeed. To turn my attention towards something besides...spilling my seed on the ground. A more metaphoric passage than literal. Waste not your efforts on self pleasure."

"Like Bob Dylan's religious phase."

"Certainly, only I knew better than to ever try it. Exhorting as such in poetry is doomed to the rubbish heap. Similarly, in your mien, I believe there are radio stations dedicated to awful, didactic pop music."

"There but for the grace."

"Aye. You see, I struggled mightily with what might seem an academic issue. Thankfully, Reverend Merton took to listening to my whining one day. 'Reg, I see your concern, I suppose,' he said, 'but your downfall here is thinking that you are such a big deal.' He excused me at that and I walked out of his office, out of the church, on to a quiet street. Another man was walking about a block away. He saw me but saw no reason to acknowledge me. I wondered if he had ever read my poems."

"Sounds pretty egotistical."

"Not this time. If he read them, I decided that they were his now, not mine. He did not read them to learn about me, he hopefully found his own life changed ever so slightly by reading them.

"So service then. We provide a service. Maybe that is a similarity."

"That would seem to be a similarity."

The two men looked at each other, comfortable with the silence, more comfortable in each other's presence than they had felt in some time. However, the time for the appointment is over.

"Forth, please come this way, sir," says Sean and heads towards the door.

"A pleasure to meet you, Forth."

"You, too Reginald."

They shake hands. Sean takes one last picture of them.

6

CARDIO *in* SPOKANE

[2002]

THE Green Paintbrush is a growing concern in Spokane. They are a new idea – a digital agency that manufactures the dreams of well-funded businesses. The company was started six years ago by Cardio Plathemy. Cardio attempted to retire to Spokane and failed to both retire and stay in Spokane. After he started The Green Paintbrush his traveling habits made it obvious to everyone that he really did not like it in Spokane.

After establishing a couple of trustworthy people to run The Green Paintbrush, Cardio moved to downtown Los Angeles. In his semi-regular phone conferences with employees of The Green Paintbrush, he usually is enthusiastically invited to come and visit and always accepts the invitation but nothing is ever put on a calendar.

Cardio made Spokane the home of a company that, on any day, may effectively and permanently influence American life. The Green Paintbrush has and continues to define the very veins through which the economy's lifeblood flows.

At the beginning of 2007, two consortiums were offering competing media formats to deliver a higher definition video than people were accustomed to. Bloomberg correctly reported one Friday that one consortium had engaged The Green Paintbrush to develop their user interface and interactivity workflow. Monday the stock price of the primary sponsor of their competitor dropped by 22%.

Cardio had tried to put the obvious out of his mind for the first few months that he lived in Spokane, but eventually he gave in to the inescapable fact that he would have to start The Green Paintbrush. He tried to just enjoy his time. At least, he did things that were the acts of someone enjoying their time. His old but utterly updated house was a wonder of architecture. The front was an imperial setting, complete with Greek columns and a full width staircase. From both the outside and the inside, his home became increasingly but not jarringly modern as you moved deeper. The back looked out onto a rolling hill and the mountains behind. Sometimes three horses grazed on that hill.

Cardio would walk in the hills around Spokane wearing absolutely natty European outdoor clothing. He would confer with the local wine merchants and vintners, stocking his cellar very selectively. He would attend local festivals.

Finally, one Spring morning he was standing before the tall, round, glass topped café table in his kitchen and looking out the window at the snow on the mountains. The scent of a nearly perfectly brewed French press coffee rose from the cup before him.

Damn. He could not do it no longer. It was simply too obvious. He took his coffee cup by the large handle and went off to find his laptop. As he was walking up a short flight of stairs he recalled that the laptop's battery was most likely dead. He would also need to find the cord.

He stopped on the stairs. He took a sip of coffee. He decided to start his new digital company on paper.

It was obvious that the world lacked the perfect digital agency even as the tools were available to make it happen. He was standing on top of the soil that would inevitably sprout one of the most powerful instruments in contemporary life and no one but for him yet understood it. The whole solution came down to one of the most basic formulas in existence.

Cardio had collected a pen and a stack of loose-leaf paper. It was unlined, but if you looked carefully you could see a faint grid of dots across the surface. When Cardio returned to his café table, he placed the stack of blank paper on the glass then pushed the three low-backed stools out of the way. Then, on the topmost page he wrote the formula:

D=RT

Distance equals rate times time. He then wrote the other two derivative formulas, each on a separate piece of paper.

R=D/T

T=D/R

His coffee had cooled slightly. A new, musty flavor was becoming apparent underneath the sharp pinch of its initial taste. He frowned and simultaneously raised his eyebrows.

The world was increasingly – and the pace of that increase was itself increasing – relying on digital communications. Secure web pages were our connection to our bank, our work, our families, recreation, socialization. Everything was currently being tried on the web or will be soon enough. Groceries, sex, love, hunting, vacationing, education, guilt, politics. All of these were traveling via wires and waves now. Although it was certain that we would need more bandwidth, expanding the wires and waves was not a very interesting problem. The correlation between investment and outcome was child's play. While hiking along a burbling mountain stream earlier in the summer, Cardio had figured out roughly, to the second decimal place, the 15-year return on network infrastructure investment. The chart, had he drawn it out, would have been a boringly consistent slope that flattens predictably as it drifts through time. Bandwidth is a commodity.

No, the problem that was more interesting was at the ends of the wires. How does someone operate a bank over the Internet? How does a grocery store expose itself to customers on their computers?

Cardio still does not feel entirely comfortable around most slow thinking people. He still tends to try what he is going to say in his mind before speaking it. Even now, in his early sixties, he peers curiously at every social process as if it was an unfamiliar species from an exotic land, growing in his garden.

He sees the process that others view as background.

It should be noted that one could say that this is exactly why Cardio has such difficulty in social situations. While he believes that he is massively smarter than others, it is apparent that he simply wastes no cognition on those things he has always been poor at, such as providing other people a handhold to relate to him. He is well dressed and well spoken, but one could come to a determination that he is actually a poor citizen of the planet who tries to compensate with a single-minded focus on an activity that he is good at, such as rock stacking.

Cardio can see transactions and relations that we have established, some through generations. How to stand in a line. How to enter a building. How to drive on a city street.

He thinks that last one and smiles. He should be writing this down, so he does.

Starting line:
Driving on a city street
Walking on a sidewalk
Entering a building
Standing in line
Having a home and returning to it

So to compute D=RT, we need to travel a distance. Where will that distance go?

Finish line:
Accomplishing something
Replacing old manner with digital comms
Home or other

Rate he knows is something of cheat, but the whole issue pivots around his connotation of the R in the formula. He is confident that the equation will hold up to his syntactical tweak.

Rate:
Adoption
Habit destruction and formation
Extinction/Absorption of old process

And then the T, a pair of determinants. He notes that this may double the complexity of the formula, which makes him smile happily.

Time:
To solution
To consumer exhaustion

Cardio covered the small table with an array of papers in the next hour. He noted that his lower back did not stiffen in the familiar way, using an elevated table.

When The Green Paintbrush opened their first office, a local manufacturer delivered a custom made circular glass-topped table whose surface was counter height, one meter off the ground.

Initially, The Green Paintbrush offered web services to local companies. Cardio knew that the size of the market had limited the quality of services available for Spokane's businesses, including the growing wine industry. Their websites needed some help.

Cardio found some moderately talented HTML programmers in the local marketplace. He secretly hired a branding company from Los Angeles to create an identity for his new company. The account manager was confused when asked to sign a confidentiality agreement before working on a small-town web design company but assented. Plop Designs did a lot of different things, but he had to admit this was his first small-market web development company image project.

Plop came up with The Green Paintbrush. Cardio was fine with anything, provided it fit the requirements he had sent over in a bulleted list.

"His list is 27 points long."

"You counted."

"Didn't you?"

"No, but I got the gist."

"What about this one: 'Positive response rate for males 35-60 in first thirty seconds of exposure'"

"This is a time and materials project. Do what you need to do."

"Do you know this guy?"

"You don't? Do you have what you need to get started?"

The name, the image, and the initial staff. Cardio assembled the business with an off-handed efficiency. His first two sales people were local boys grown up. The first few clients were restaurants and bars in the downtown area. His web developers made professional, contemporary websites for the clients. The clients were happy. Cardio was barely paying attention. He told the sales guys to land wineries, and then Cardio went to University.

He timed his visit for late in the summer as the leadership faculty assembled their course offerings. Only a few students witnessed him walking across the Spokane River and up to the Herak Center.

When he showed up for his appointment, Cardio carried a duplicate of the packet he had sent to the chair of the Mathematics department:

CV, a proposed syllabus, a letter of recommendation from the head of the Stanford University School of Business. The chair was happy to accommodate Cardio's course. He was having trouble filling enough non-major classes as it was. This was a perfect course for all of those soft-minded communications students.

Next term, it appeared in the course catalog with this description:

> **MATH 247: The Mathematics of Communication**
> Non-major elective course. Mathematics in application to the principles of mass communication, emphasis on linear and non-linear equations as a method for quantifying the principles of communication systems.

7

TEACHING

[2002]

THIS was not the first class Cardio stood before. The recommendation from Stanford that he brought to the dean was genuine. He was asked to teach a statistics course a few years ago. It was inauspicious. The students and the teacher quickly developed mutual disinterest. The Dean of the Stanford School of Business enjoyed Cardio's presence at cocktail parties and felt that the reviews and outcomes of the class itself were of little import.

Having read a case study on Clear and Sane Roads, the Dean also felt that Cardio was something of a VIP in the world of business. A most obscure type of VIP, that referencing him showed deep knowledge of minutiae. Knowing Cardio personally was still more impressive. He was happy to write the letter recommending Cardio for this northerly school.

So on a bright fall day in Spokane 2002, Cardio walked back into the Herak Center, heading for his own classroom and a pack of 22 young Americans varying in age from 19 to 26. He tried to focus on acting like a teacher.

When this all began, at his breakfast table, fueled by the new idea, he had written a plan for the course, complete with books and references. The books were directly from his own shelf or the important books of his youthful study.

He got a little sentimental when he discovered that a foundational statistics survey he had dog-eared in college was now out of print.

Looking up at the mountain from his table, the mountain gleaming under a blazing noontime sun, Cardio said aloud, "Maybe I will be a good teacher."

He found it helpful to reflect on that moment as he walked into the classroom. He had notes for his own reference and he had his printed syllabus to hand out. Two of the younger students had brought all of the books on his reading list to class and had even stacked them in a tapering tower on their desks.

"Hello. My name is Cardio Plathemy and I am your teacher for this class, Mathematics of Communication. If this is not the class you meant to be in...too bad for you. Drop that class tomorrow. Stay here with us today."

Cardio's voice was very even, as it tends to be. He paused for a long time, waiting. He consciously pushed the charming smile across his face that had cued appropriate laughter in the past. It was moderately successful this time as well. He pushed the stack of papers forward on to the desk and pointed at the woman in the frontmost rightmost (from his perspective) desk.

"Please pass around this syllabus and I will introduce the course." She was a little taken aback at being asked to rise, but did as she was told. He watched as she took the stack and split it in two at his table. She then took the two stacks back to her desk. One she handed to the woman behind her and one she handed to the young man to her right.

"Interesting," said Cardio. He seemed to not know that he spoke out loud. Returning to his own mind for a moment, Cardio took a small notepad out of his bag. He sketched a grid and drew arrows from one corner to both directions and wrote "outcome?"

He realized that he should have been talking to the class at this point. Leaving the notepad open on his lectern, he made eye contact briefly with several members of the class and started into his remarks.

"Over the all too brief semester, we will cover the mathematical basis for a variety of communication modes, observed in situ as best we can.

"This will probably involve algebra, algebraic geometry, and some trigonometry. As you noticed, there is no specific math prerequisite for this course. Rather, I have assigned books that can help us to derive the appropriate formulas, and then solve them as best they can be solved. There are no actual reading assignments, all of the books are optional."

He was not aware, and had he been aware he would have viewed it as insignificant to all outcomes, that his books totaled $42 when purchased from the University bookstore.

"The syllabus before you is the best that I could offer you for structure in the course. I considered organizing this class as a chronological survey of communications methods, but then I was not so sure that such an organization would build a good cognitive experience in the student. You see, the assumption would be that we would move from simple to complex, as that is the traditional direction of a college course. However, the equation of an early novel might not build upon and increase complexity from a cave drawing. I was concerned that we would not have a cohesive experience and you would leave class on the last day slowly shaking your head, cursing my very name under your breath.

"So you can see that the syllabus is a listing in table form. The first column is the week of our semester. The second column is the year, date, or era of the subject that we will cover. The third is a short title, and the fourth – the widest column – is a short explanation.

"I am not very happy with the syllabus, because it does not illustrate a progression, nor the relationship between these items. It could just as easily be a grocery list of unlike items. Apples, refried beans, 5W-30 motor oil. No, it is a bad syllabus. So, our first task today is to make a new syllabus that will provide you with some more information about what I am going to do with this class.

"If the class was perfectly chronological, I could have made a timeline. A timeline is of course a one-dimensional chart, simply an x axis. As such, the only directions to travel are up and down. The primary method of moving along it would be to add or subtract."

Cardio felt some gratitude when he took up a dry erase marker and turned toward the board. For a time, his face relaxed from the series of practiced facial expressions. He drew a very clean and straight horizontal line near to the bottom of the dry erase board. Having freehanded tables and charts for a lifetime, Cardio's steady hand could pinstripe a kilometer-long train without a waver. He placed perfectly vertical hash marks at even intervals across the line.

"However, since this class is not chronological, we need to express the 'class time' in another manner. I need to introduce another dimension, another axis." He proceeded to draw a vertical line up from the center of the x axis. "This also represents time, but it represents our class time, the fifteen weeks we will spend together in this cozy little room.

"Today, our first incident is already happening; we are looking at our own syllabus as an item to analyze. So, the first item to plot is in the top right; week 1 day 1 intersected with the present day, 2002." After putting a large dot on the upper right of the board, he turned toward the class, "And what is your name, sir?" The dry erase pen extending with astounding accuracy to indicate a young man in a broad-striped polo top. Green and white. He had short cropped blonde hair sprouting in a carefully haphazard manner. Cardio chose him because he was in the middle of the class and was looking directly at the board as Cardio turned.

"Phillip." Phillip has a surprisingly husky voice.

"Phillip Phillip Phillip. You must all understand that I frequently fail to recall names of acquaintances. Soon, we will all be very close friends. However, please have patience with me as our relationship grows and strengthens. We can all laugh together at my little failings as a teacher. I am a little rough around the edges, but will strive to improve. So, Phillip, can you help me and let me know what the next item is on the syllabus? The next row in the poor table on the paper before you?"

"The probability of cave drawing and petroglyphs."

"Oh dear. That is a long ways back." He wrote '38,000 BC' on the far left of the x axis, then reached up and drew a gently downward sloping line from the syllabus dot to a point high above 38,000 BC. OK. Now Philip, what is the next stop?"

"Broadside distribution in revolutionary America."

"Thank you Philip." A hash is assigned 1770, a dot is placed above it, and the line snakes back to the right. "Well, you can see how this is going. Interesting, eh? Now we have three points, we can compute the distance traveled along both axes, we can compute how steep the slope is, we can identify angles. We can do math." He took up a green pen and highlighted elements across the two axis timeline.

"Your first assignment: for the next class, I would like for everyone to recreate this and finalize it as a presentation-quality chart. Then, express that depiction in words."

A mousy boy raised his hand and simultaneously asked, "how many pages?"

"What is your name, sir?"

"Roy."

"Roy, Roy, Roy. Use as many words as you need but as few as possible." Cardio put down the dry erase marker, picked up his pen, and made a three-word entry into the small notepad that was still sitting on the lectern. "Roy in box."

"So, I have been somewhat sneaky here. I have taken the explanation of the syllabus and made it a lesson. But please, let me return to the business of learning and ask you now if there are any questions about the syllabus? Any concerns?"

"What will you test us on?" Roy again. Cardio marks a hash next to "Roy in box." He underlined the phrase as well.

"That is yet to be determined. Any other questions?" Cardio focused his eyes on Roy, hoping that it would cause the boy to shrink and not follow up.

"Well how can we prepare if we don't know what the test is?" A second hash mark. With your naked eye you could see that this one stretched slightly longer than the previous one. With a microscope, you could see that the pen dug significantly deeper into the paper.

Cardio's voice turned cold, "I would suggest that you attend class and listen to your teacher. Does anyone else have any questions or comments on the syllabus?" He was pretty certain that the vicious tone would prevent further derailments, and he was correct. After a brief silence that held only Roy's loud, embarrassed breathing, Cardio wrapped up.

"Well, since there are no other questions, I look forward to working with all of you on Thursday but I am happy to give over the rest of this class time to your other indulgences. Class dismissed." Cardio flipped the notebook closed and put it into his bag. The rightmost frontmost woman had stood up, picked up a heavily stuffed backpack and put it on her chair. She was unzipping it when Cardio stepped around the table and put his hand on the surface of her desk to get her attention.

"And what is your name?"

"Cherry." Cherry wore her blonde hair long, past her shoulder, with longish bangs. If you got the impression that she had the same hairstyle since middle school, you would be correct. She wore cargo pants and a fashionable top, highlighted with some sort of metallic glitter.

"Cherry, forgive me, I am not normally a teacher. Can you tell me if it would be unusual for me to ask to glance at your notes?"

She looked at him sidelong, "No teacher has asked me that before, but you may." She had closed the cheap green vinyl portfolio around her legal pad and had it in her hand already. She handed it, still closed, to Cardio. Cherry kept her eyes on his face while he flipped it open.

"I noticed that you took four pages of notes during the class and I was curious, as a method of ascertaining the experience of attending the lecture, if I could find out what content you felt fit to record."

Cherry's handwriting was a scrawl, a code for only her. The more interesting code was how she used the page. Instead of writing across the page from margin to margin, her page was populated with rectangles and circles. They varied in height but took up either the entire width, 2/3 of the page, or 1/3 of the page. Generally sticking to the cardinal directions, lines traveled the page.

The last of the class was clogged at the door, squeezed from disorder to a single file path through the door, and then chaotically in varying directions, manner, and pace. Cardio looked up and considered fluid dynamics briefly.

Soon only Cardio and Cherry were left in the room.

"What does the darkening of the contact point here and here signify?" Cardio asked.

Cherry had one hand in her backpack, holding the place the portfolio belonged. "Those are relationships that could become discussion or essay. There seems to be something to examine."

"And the corkscrew right before some connection points?"

"Connections that I made, not a part of the lecture."

"Very interesting, Cherry. You always take notes like this?" Cardio handed back the open portfolio. Cherry had to take her hand out of her backpack so that she could take the floppy thing from his hand and close it.

"Yes, mostly."

"Have a lovely day, Cherry cherry cherry." Cardio returned to his lectern to gather his own bag. Cherry noted that he took the small notebook back out of the bag, flipped it open expertly, and wrote a brief couple of lines.

8

the GREEN PAINTBRUSH

[2010]

AFTER leaning his bike against the window behind his desk, Reginald walked to the front of his workstation and pressed the power button on his computer. Two screens flickered and the fans started to hum. He walked towards the kitchen to get a cup of coffee.

The large, airy room was blessed with vaulted ceilings. Unlike many of these old buildings, this floor had never been subjected to drop ceilings of acoustical tile. The stone of the exterior walls cradled the tall, arched windows.

A continuous two-sided desk weaved its way through the space. Twice it stretched two thirds of the distance from the wall towards the elevator, curved 180 degrees, and headed back to the vaulted glass behind it. A few workstations with one, two, or three monitors claimed space on the desktop.

In one corner, the windows huddled around three bright green couches formed in a triangle with extremely narrow aisles between them. Next to them, towards the elevators, was an unusually tall, rather large, round glass table.

The opposite corner has three glass doors with large windows between them, a clear partition into two separate ecosystems. Two contain large tables, one of which has a projector crouching upon it. The third door has venetian blinds pulled down and turned to their most extreme downward angle.

There is a fair amount of space, maybe five meters, between the elevator door and the desk snake. The Green Paintbrush has no reception area. Reginald, when he is the first person to work, sometimes tries to think of what the effect of entering this space is, with classic architecture and inconveniently contemporary furnishings. If NASA set up offices in Notre Dame Cathedral? A colony of hyper intelligent ants burrowing into St. Petersburg? Perhaps from the inside out; an overly-funded startup run by an eccentric fan of Gothic novels.

He liked the contrast, and felt comfortable here. He wondered briefly if he would miss it. "Probably no," he said out loud.

He was not the only person here just now. In fact, Reginald was rather late to arrive this morning. He had not awakened particularly late, perhaps the time spent writing or the time spent bothering with an old lost memory delayed him. Perhaps he rode more slowly than usual to work this morning. It did not matter and he tried to not spend time thinking through his solitary morning, now past. The Green Paintbrush was waves of activity.

A small stereo played Johnny Cash "Ring of Fire." A pair of women sat near a vertex of the couches. One held a 16 ounce paper coffee cup in both of her hands. She nodded while the other woman gesticulated and spoke quite loudly. They leaned in towards each other.

Several workstations glowed. A bearded man in his late twenties wearing giant full-coverage headphones held his face close to the middle of his three monitors, clutching a mouse like it was a gearshift.

Through the middle conference room window, Reginald could see three people leaning in to the conference call speakerphone set in the middle of the table. A fourth was standing, poised with a dry erase pen. They all looked like they were holding their breath.

It is a beautiful place, thought Reginald. I will miss it. No. I won't miss it. But I will remember it. Yes. It is a beautiful place, and I will remember it. His stomach felt shellacked, hard and reflective.

He had been greeted by several of these people as he pushed his bike around the desk snake and headed back towards the kitchen, a large alcove beside the elevators. He felt that his responses were appropriate each time. As he approached the kitchen, he saw that Cherry was standing in front of the microwave, holding a spoon. Instead of looking at her, he checked the readout on the microwave. It was ticking down from 4:23.

Four minutes and twenty seconds is a long time. He and Cherry had sex eleven days prior. He touched the bridge of his nose. It was still a little sensitive on the right side where she had hit him. Either she is left handed or he was holding her right arm down, he is not sure which. Sex does not feel like the right word. They fucked. Or something.

The Green Paintbrush has a sophisticated single cup coffee maker that grinds and brews a cup of coffee to order. All of the instructions are pictographs of smaller cups, larger cups, and cups with some sort of swirl above it. To make a cup of coffee, place a cup below the hopper, push a pictogram, then push the glowing green button. It takes one to two minutes for the coffee to be ready.

“Hi Cherry.” “Hi Reginald.” They spoke not quite simultaneously. He managed to start greeting her before she greeted him. She shifted her weight towards the door.

After the happy hour that Friday, the two of them had found common cause to seek out a television showing the end of a particular college basketball game and headed off together to another bar away from the rest of The Green Paintbrush crowd. They ended up in a bar pocked with television screens and tall tables. On a busy Friday night, they managed to find a small, tall table, but all the stools had been claimed by a swelling party adjacent. They stood and leaned on the table, shoulder to shoulder.

“Sports, Cardio Style.” She said. A waitress came up to them. Cherry and Reginald looked at each other then ordered strong, daring drinks.

Three rounds of strong, daring drinks later, they were embracing in celebration of the miracle win, the kind of ending that no script can manage as well as a pitched battle. They were embracing. She was wearing a tank top with thin straps, her bra straps also visible. She hugged him at first around the neck in celebration then opened her elbows over his shoulders. Something shifted in her muscles. He could feel something shifting. He moved his hands lower, to the small of her back that he admired so much. They stopped yelling and stopped bouncing. Something else. Swaying. Drunk.

Waiting for a cab in Spokane is a tricky proposition. They are not a professional corps of drivers; it is not a competitive marketplace. The potential customers are often left out in the cold for quite some time. They translate the careful vagaries of the dispatcher however they want and stay in one place, peeking all directions in hopes a lit car will appear and end their purgatory.

Reginald and Cherry were outside of the corner bar. He was leaning his back against the cold, stone wall. She was leaning against him, shivering. He kept his arms around her. She moved her shoulders against him and sometimes arched her back into his chest. When he had his hands on her stomach he felt her deep and measured breathing, punctuated sometimes by a quiver. He was wearing a corduroy long sleeved shirt, perfect for this weather. However, he was not wearing any undershirt. He could not offer it to her.

He liked holding her. It was sobering and he was in need of sobering. He leaned his head down into the pocket of her neck and shoulder. Gave her something like a kiss there.

When the cab came and the moment broke she said something and they were both laughing he turned out and reached ahead and opened the back door for her then slid in after.

"Warmth!" She said, shivering one more time. He remembers that; she had crossed her bare arms to rub her forearms. He was definitely smiling large and felt like he was watching her on television.

The rest was like flipping through the channels. He was never able to remember certain connecting details. She must have given the cab driver her address because they went to her house. He does not remember who paid for the ride, or leaving the cab. Something about entering her house, about choosing a glass from her cupboard and getting water from the tap, checking the temperature with his finger. She was laughing again, behind him. Leaning against the stove. As an experiment, he has thought about it and has no memory of ever hearing her laugh again.

He does remember kissing in the kitchen, laughing and kissing then just kissing. Her naked stomach, on the bed. A firm handful of breast. Her eyes opened very, very wide. He remembers that. Her expression was so unusual. His arm engaged, hand wrapped around her wrist. Not much more comes to mind before leaving, stepping out of her front door, turning the lock before he closed it behind himself.

When writing and speaking, some people say that their life – the matters of the world collected from their senses and made sense of by their mind – is a river that flows through time. At other times, the same person may speak of existence as a vast ocean that an individual's senses and cognition explores, directionless.

Reginald used to think that it was lazy to move between these two metaphors without discernment. He would extend both metaphors to idiocy in his mind: A river flowing through the ocean, the metaphorical salmon, Life's Estuary.

Both metaphors work under particular conditions. He turns to the coffee maker. It is not appropriate for him to start any conversation with Cherry that is not purely related to work. It is not appropriate for him to act particularly friendly. She has made this clear.

No one else is in the kitchen. "I am resigning today," Reginald says to the coffee maker. It interrupts him with a clatter and hiss.

"Excuse me?" Cherry said.

I am resigning today. I am going to leave town and I hope that this is the right thing for you, but I will do it anyway. He looks at the doorway. "I am leaving."

"Well, you can go ahead and finish making your coffee first," Cherry says.

He has to step towards her, which he did not want to do. "No, I mean I am leaving Spokane."

"Ah." That is all she said. The two stood bracketed by the rumble of the microwave and the hoarse yell of the coffee maker, facing not at each other. When the coffee finished, Reginald nodded to her and left. He needed to print out his letter of resignation and deliver it.

Back at his workstation, Reginald inserted a thirty-minute meeting on the schedule for Blaine, the operations manager, and the smaller conference room. Then, he called up the resignation letter that he had carefully crafted two evenings prior. After making sure that there was not anyone hanging around the shared printer, he pressed print. He rose from his chair, walked to the printer to collect the single page, then returned to his chair. He put the paper face down on his desk, took a sip of coffee, and started working.

Reginald is a user experience engineer. Not designer, engineer. Cardio insisted that the word "design" not be used for the marketing or address of Green Paintbrush projects.

“Design is soft and unscientific,” Cardio had gathered Cherry and the rest of his first true user experience staff, one year after the initial launch of The Green Paintbrush. “Engineering is based upon specifications and proofs. You are engineers. Engineers are turned to for expert insight. Designers are rolled over in the face of other considerations. Engineering starts early in a project and design happens late, as budget and time allows.”

Cardio had to overcome a personal academic bugaboo to adopt engineer and engineering for his company's lexicon; there was a time when engineer could not be affixed to anyone not specifically trained and tested. Cardio missed that time, missed people dressing for work, missed musicians who chose the title “entertainer” over “artist.” That set of values had no further effect on the future. He quieted the desire for the past as best he could and affixed conjugations of engineer to every aspect of The Green Paintbrush.

Perhaps to alleviate his guilt, he designed a brief curriculum for new Green Paintbrush engineers that served as a certification of sorts.

When going head to head with design firms, The Green Paintbrush engineers landed the meaty and significant projects while the designers were asked to do too little, too late, with too few resources.

Reginald had been assigned to rethink an ATM. Today was his first day of three dedicated solely to reconsider how to perform banking operations simply. He had an hour before his meeting with Blaine. He closed all the open applications on his computer except for a sparse text editor. After expanding that window to full screen, he leaned back and looked at the white expanse.

Each engineer at The Green Paintbrush took pride in having their own process, their own medium. For Reginald, it came down to bare, unformatted text. Digital, not handwritten. When he would have lunch with other engineers or kill time before conference calls, he would say that the digital words are more neutral, that they are more honest. In reality, he preferred to preserve handwritten words for his more personal work. It was a sentimental reason. He started to write criteria for how to bank more efficiently.

9

CARDIO *and* CARS

[1982]

CARDIO went car shopping. In 1982, driving was still a powerful and constant part of American life. Normal people purchased high-performance cars and used them to commute in thick traffic. What make and model of car you drove informed people of your identity. Choosing your own was an effort in matching your self perception with your pocket book while making some allowances for your actual functional requirements.

Cardio had noted this but did not participate. However, to design insurance for a new world, he felt a need to become more immersed in driving culture.

Mornings were crisp and bright this time of year in Salt Lake City. Cardio drove up Interstate 15 towards the Temple and a cluster of car lots. He pulled in to a BMW dealership. Cardio was driving a five-year old BMW 320i.

Brady was standing outside in the sun. He was underdressed for the cold morning, wearing lighter colored clothes, a thin jacket and light shoes. He had just finished a cigarette but remained outside in the sun, empty handed for a time. Cardio's 320i passed by where Brady stood and parked at the main entrance.

Brady had been a car salesman for two and a half months. His first month had been pretty good. The second, not as great. This month was a worry for him. As a car salesman, what can he do to soothe these concerns but stand here in the sun, on the lot?

This is shit. Then again, this is all perfect. If you are going to be in Salt Lake City early in the winter, here is work of a sort that means standing and gathering in the already powdered mountains with your eyes. There is not much you can do to improve your fate on a morning like this but breathe.

Brady was good at breathing. When possible, in the last few weeks as it has gotten cold, he had stood there in the morning light, south of the door facing southeast and breathing. Sometimes, after chucking his cigarette, he would close his eyes. At 25 years old, this was not his last stop. This was his current waterfall.

Brady watched Cardio scan for a parking place and head around the corner of the building, towards the front door. Brady closed his eyes for one more brief moment and then turned and walked toward Cardio, who was exiting his car.

"Hello there. How is your day getting on?" Brady said.

"Hello." Cardio was holding his small notebook, tucking it into his jacket pocket after closing the car door. He tapped his heart to confirm that there was a pen clipped in his breast pocket.

The morning light and the two men's breaths frolicked around their heads, catching each other and then fading.

Brady tapped his plastic nametag. He hated the nametag. "I'm Brady, what are you looking for?"

"I want to look at some cars, please," said Cardio.

"We have some that you can look at, for sure. It is a bit cold here. I was going to get a cup of coffee inside. Care for one, or a cider if you prefer?"

"Certainly," Cardio was trying to present certain typical car-buyer actions, and he felt that accepting a free cup of coffee – regardless of the quality of that coffee – was inline with his character.

Inside, they passed between two cars, one a convertible with the top down and the other a four-door sedan. Brady and Cardio walked at an easy pace together. Neither spoke until they got to the coffee maker. Brady was still thinking about his breathing. He inverted two cups from the tower of cups and poured coffee into both.

"Cream or sugar?" he indicated the variety of single serve packets on the table. Cardio's lip tensed slightly, but it was hardly perceptible.

"No. Thank you." The cups had cardboard wings that could be folded out to act as a finger loop. Neither Brady nor Cardio used these, "Can you tell me about…this car here?" Cardio indicated towards the two cars in the showroom. His arm hovered between them for a moment, then pointed at the convertible.

"That is the 318i convertible coupe. Lovely little number. Were you interested in moving into a convertible?"

"Do you sell a lot of those here?"

"Sure. Lot's of successful people snap them up." Brady was thinking about the loops on the cup again. Every time he poured one of these cups he thought about the loops. Almost no one ever used them. Children with hot cocoa. There was a particular type of person who did. He remembered that a couple had come in to look for a third car for the family. Cliff and Henrietta's eldest son was getting old enough to drive and so they were going to buy a car for Henrietta. Their son would get the hand me down. Cliff took the cup with his apple cider in it and delicately held it by the bottom at eye level to inspect the wings. He pulled them out one at a time and put his index finger through it.

Brady had already noticed that when you employ the fold-out finger hole, the cup sags and you are forced to brace a lower finger against the hot surface. Cliff put that finger there, then as the back of that finger started to warm, placed the first two fingers of his other hand under the base of the cup to prop it up. He cradled the cup at his sternum. Henrietta and Brady both held their cups with their respective thumbs on the rim and their fingers on the base, skipping the fold-out finger hole entirely. Cliff and Henrietta bought the 318i convertible.

Cardio did not walk towards the car. He pulled his cup towards his face to use his upper lip to gauge the temperature, and then lowered the cup. Brady noticed that Cardio had a large hand. His thumb and forefinger splayed across the rim of the cup. His pinkie and ring finger served as a platform. Cardio had not responded but was looking about the room.

The room was shiny. Morning light was filling up the bank of windows across the entrance. The floor, particularly this early in the morning, reflected wavy editions of the two cars through its creamy surface. A lectern with a thick catalog stood at the right turn signal of each car. Each lectern was oak that had been finished and polished to a sheen. The catalog, should you approach it, gleamed as well. Without thinking, you would have to move your head back and forth to alter the placement of your own head and the bursts from the light fixtures when trying to read or make out the pictures explaining each car.

"How many people do you talk to each day, Brady? Here, in the showroom."

"Total? It varies. Sometimes two. Sometimes a dozen."

"And they don't all buy cars?"

"Oh, no. Heavens no."

"What do they ask about?"

"There are men who want to talk about engineering details. Very minute stuff. Usually, they know things about the car that I do not. I listen and am enthusiastic. There are other men that want to talk about resale value and life of engine and repairs. I offer them assurances. It works pretty well to just say 'that's a good question.'"

"Does anybody tell you what they need the car to do?" Cardio lifted the coffee again to his lip to check the temperature. Still too hot.

Brady thought for a second. He noticed that he ever so briefly held his breath while he took a second to recall. "I will tell you the truth, Cardio. I have not been here that long, but no. I don't recall that happening. People don't tell me what they want the car to do."

"Should not that be the source of criteria for purchasing a car?"

Brady smacked his lips then inhaled while tilting his head to the side. "Well, I suppose they don't buy a car because it is nice to sit in during a traffic jam. Maybe they want the car to bring some beauty into their life. They just can't bring themselves to tell me that about such a big expenditure."

"So it would seem." Cardio checked the coffee temperature and this time he took a small sip. "Thank you, Brady. I am not interested in buying a car today." He felt it was polite to take the coffee with him, though he had no intention of drinking any more. At the car lot's exit, he opened his car door a crack and poured the coffee out.

10

RESIGNING

[2010]

CARDIO was fortunate or skilled enough to have established a nearly perfect operations manager at The Green Paintbrush. Blaine had moved to Spokane from Seattle after having moved to Seattle from San Francisco. This cultural downsizing had taken around five years.

Blaine is now in his mid or perhaps late forties. He has thus far resisted the urge to purchase and wear comfortable but unstylish clothing or end his subscriptions to cultural magazines. Everybody refers to Blaine as a rock star and he refers to everybody around him as a rock star.

Once every couple of months Blaine flies to Los Angeles to meet with Cardio and have dinner with people. He likes these short, hot bursts of truly urban time.

Every morning Blaine drives in to Spokane from his acreage of orchards east of town. Blaine, his wife, and their young daughter live out there; about a half hour drive from downtown Spokane. This morning, Blaine had left as the sunrise was mirrored on his bay windows, broken up by the roughened wood trim between the four windows. The orange colors shared a pigment with the wood. He was very happy to pause for just a moment, lean against the back door of his small sport utility vehicle and look at the sunrise projected against his home. After watching for a while with his arms crossed, he pulled out his phone and snapped a picture.

Five minutes before the meeting with Reginald, Blaine was working on an email to all Green Paintbrush employees that would be sent Tuesday of the following week. Blaine's inbox was a well-tended garden, his calendar a clean room. His cell phone and his computer dinged in quick succession. He finished the email that he was writing, which took five minutes, then saved it as a draft. He checked his inbox and archived three new irrelevant items. He had five minutes until the meeting. He opened the new picture of his house from his cell phone and posted it to his public photo gallery on the Internet. Then he folded his laptop closed and rose to meet Reginald in the small conference room. The meeting's subject was "Face To Face."

"What's up, Reg?"

Reginald looked down at the paper in his hand and pushed it forward. "I did not want to email this to you."

Blaine turned the paper 180 degrees by twirling it with one finger and read the first half, then looked up at Reginald. "OK."

"My current projects will carry through to the end of the month. I would like to continue until then."

"OK. Can I throw you a going away party?"

"Sure."

"Did you see the sunrise today?"

"Don't recall it, Blaine. Probably not."

Blaine cued up the picture he took that morning on his phone and pointed the screen at Reginald.

"Nice."

"Where are you going? Should I worry about your non-compete?" Blaine smiled and chuckled. Reginald smiled back. Nobody at The Green Paintbrush signed a non-compete contract, just an agreement to not utilize recognizable Green Paintbrush Process in the execution of projects. Cardio wanted clients to believe that system and process, not talent, delivered the project. He never performed well when fenced in, and did not expect that his employees would either.

Reginald was pretty sure that he was going to Charleston. He had a phone interview a few days earlier and liked the idea of moving to someplace that old.

"Not sure yet. Time to move away, I think."

Blaine waited for more information. Reginald waited for the end of the meeting. When they parted, Blaine went to his office and revised the email to include an invite to Reginald's going away party.

No one at The Green Paintbrush noticed a change, or at least never enough to comment, after the night that Reginald and Cherry watched that game together. When a person is motivated, bile can be staunched. A broken soul evolves into a great dramatist. Both Cherry and Reginald managed some great stints on stage since then, sometimes in shared scenes. They came together for these dramas, improvising masterfully a continuity that was, in actuality, broken and not mending.

For Cherry, there is no question how most every moment with Reginald was traumatic. She would not think thoroughly about it, unwilling to think about it deeply or allow it to remain on the front of her mind for any extended time. She had come to no conclusions about what to do, about how to solve the problem. Until she may solve the problem, she felt that leaving every other part of her life – work, friends, home – as untouched as possible seemed the best course. Thus her acting job.

Reginald did his best to not look directly at Cherry, because when he did he started to think that, incomprehensibly, he was evil. It was rare that he could overcome his belief that it was impossible for him to be evil, be the source of evil with no corollary, the origin with no partner. By acting in a world unchanged, he lifted his mind above these difficult thoughts.

Both of them had found that working was a good resort when their thoughts became too tangled. Today, Reginald walked back to his desk. Before he sat down, he whipped his mouse back and forth. The screen started to lighten and was fully awake by the time he sat down.

The entire screen was white, with one sentence across the top in a small, serif font.

Banking is only algorithms;

He edited it to read

Banking is an algorithm; (D=RT).

11

HOMEWORK

[2002]

THIS semester, the start of her fourth year, her eighth semester counting the previous summer that she stayed in Spokane, Cherry felt some need to declare a major. It felt like a great sacrifice.

There had been a few unfocused classes in a variety of different subjects. The accrued credits fell into an increasingly large pile that, until she declared a major of some sort, had to be considered elective.

Upon consideration of any one class she was slowed when thinking of saying goodbye to all of the other courses. She wormed her way into upper division math, literature, and social sciences on the back of her diverse prerequisites. To consider declaring one direction and arranging her classes for the rest of her time at school was uninteresting.

Once again, this semester she had selected a range of courses that made no sense to her general advisor. Cherry avoided her general advisor. This semester she had finagled a signature without too much back and forth by scheduling their meeting right before lunch and then appearing late. Diedre protested only slightly, but gave up the needed ink onto Cherry's registration. Cherry got the classes she wanted.

Along with Cardio's class, she was taking a 300 level literature class titled "Shakespeare and The Bible," a class on filmmaking, and the same Biology course as a pre-med friend of hers.

The first of Cardio's Mathematics of Communication class sessions was on a Tuesday. Wednesday night Cherry was in the computer lab.

She had a notebook containing the syllabus. It was covered in pen ink. She had scared up a tablet of grid-printed paper and had splayed several pages of marked up charts around the workstation that she claimed.

Cherry talked to think, and now she was talking to the machine in front of her, "This is only two dimensions, we can represent it in a couple of ways, with the class time a constant or the historic timeline a constant. Basically we can invert it and see the same information representing different information. I guess the same *data* representing different information."

She was not yet great at making computers do what she needed – and computers were not yet good at doing what they were told – but she had taken some programming classes and taught herself some of the dominant applications for previous classes. She sat there for two hours. She opened a bunch of windows on the screen, she stood at the printer as faulty print jobs spewed multiple pages of garbage characters. Eventually, as the lab was closing, she devised a method for presenting her version of the syllabus. She used images pasted into Microsoft PowerPoint slides.

It may be hard to recall but in 2002 data was hard to come by. We were surprised that one could get turn by turn directions from one place in America to another from a website, so fast that clearly a person had not been involved in the process. Students and workers at the university were allocated fifteen megabytes for the storage of their email. Normal digital image resolution was quite low, to save bandwidth and to accommodate an 800 by 600 pixel monitor.

Slide 1 was a recreation of the table presentation that Cardio handed out. She hand entered that data into a spreadsheet and then into a table in PowerPoint, here an easily formatted state that was readable, but sadly could do no other work.

Slide 2 was a finalized version of the table that Cardio had started to sketch out on the board, with historic time across the bottom and class time across the vertical axis.

Slide 3 was those two axes reversed.

Slide 4 was a table of the time differential between items, the text color coded blue for moving forward in time and red for moving backward.

Slide 5 was a pie chart of the mediums covered: paper, architecture, computer data.

She printed out her images, placed them in the inside pocket of her plastic portfolio, and left the lab.

It was 10 pm and Cherry had been in the lab since sunset. The Eastern Washington winter was starting to make itself known. She had under-dressed again, wearing a pink short-sleeved polo shirt and no jacket. Her forearms prickled and tightened. Cherry felt her legs hurry to get her away from the discomfort. In response, she willed herself to slow a bit. The cold was not deadly, her dorm was only ten minutes away.

Her neck was bare and she started to feel the cold curling under her collar. She noticed that her left hand went into the pocket of her jeans. Her right hand was holding the portfolio downward but flipped it up against her arm so that it could press her fingers into the side of her leg.

She tried to figure out how much it improved her relative warmth to sandwich these fingers between vinyl and denim. She noted that it made her aware of the cold on the back of her hand and that it wanted to go into a pocket like the left hand.

"Good thing I did not remember to bring a jacket," She said out loud and smiled. Her jaw convulsed from the cold.

Cherry should be accustomed to cold. Cherry could say that she came from a small, Midwestern town. However, that may conjure a far more romantic image than her home town could possibly muster. It was not Our Town or a black and white film starring Jimmy Stewart. Her town was a small and still-shrinking population that made their way around a collection of corrugated metal and old Airstream trailers. One small house had, in the course of ten years, been converted to a chicken coop and then back into a house. She grew up there with her mom and eventually her much younger half brother, whom she always simply called her brother.

She knew well enough that mentioning her small town had particular effects on people's behavior. Now, in college, she had a single delivery that worked pretty well. Later on in her life she developed a couple of different ways of phrasing her origin story that worked for different audiences and achieved different results.

Tonight, as she came out of the cold and into her dormitory, Jack was in the television lounge. She sat next to him for a while. While she sat, she squeezed the portfolio between her hands with diagonal corners pressed into each palm. She used her fingers to idly spin it, then attempted to keep it spinning with an up and down motion of her arms.

Eventually she and Jack went up to her room.

12

GOING AWAY PREPARATIONS

[2010]

TWO weeks before his last day at The Green Paintbrush, Reginald found a hand-addressed letter in an envelope of high quality paper in his mailbox. It was of such high quality that only someone who concerns himself with the quality of stationery – such as Reginald – would notice how expensive it is. The embossed "C.P." on the flap was not tinted. It would easily be missed by a more hurried, less appreciative recipient.

Reginald is more apt to check his mail than many 25 year-olds in 2010. Like most, he has his paycheck directly deposited to an account. The automated letter he receives twice a month is merely a notification that the electronic transaction has taken place.

He spent some time with that letter this month, re-reading it and marking it with a blue pen.

Rcginald rcccivcs thc bulk of his bills via cmail and pays thcm through an online portal.

This process has been most fascinating to him of late.

But, since he occasionally manages to submit poems to periodicals, he does check his physical mailbox several times a week. As his hand turns the key in the uniform apartment complex secured postal center, he will have an idle hope that a dramatic change is about to happen. Before that sense can be moderated by a calculation of exactly how little effect a publication would have on his life, he has rifled through the automatically produced letters and determined that nothing of the sort will happen today.

Today, he opens the finely milled envelope. Reginald has never received a hand written letter from Cardio, so he does not recognize the handwriting. In fact, apart from a rare bulk email to all employees, he had not received any direct communication from his nominal boss. Inside, he found multiple pages of a matching cotton paper and another envelope.

My Dear Mr. Cashon;

Enclosed in the second envelope is a letter of reference. You may realize right now that it is two-fold pointless: you have (I understand) already found new employment and paper letters of recommendation have little place in today's hiring practices. Nonetheless, I recommend that you maintain this in your records. There are further adventures and this is a light tool to carry with you. It may become useful, perhaps to start a fire on a cold night. For me, it is an expression not of gratitude but of appreciation.

There are some obvious things that I could point out at this point: you have eight letters in your first name. Your age is currently a multiple of five. Your new employer is plumbing opportunities in industries with negative growth that are seeking ever-more refined efficiencies to stave off the terror of total transformation. Now that I have pointed out those more obvious facts in a suitably oblique manner, let me express an appreciation of what is within the numbers, that sews the numbers together, and that is more than the numbers.

You needn't share this fact (I would strongly prefer that you do not, and I know that your habit is to remain somewhat restrained in your sharing so I have some confidence that this confidence will be maintained) but I read and view everything that everyone at The Green Paintbrush produces. Apart from Cherry, your efforts are the most resonant that I come across. I could thank you for all of your work for my company, but that would be the gratitude I am not writing about. I must focus on the appreciation.

In less than two years in Spokane, Reginald, you have found a consistent pulse that can be picked out of the cacophony at every corner of this country. That pulse is found – or corollaries, or reactive antitheses – in every developed country. Perhaps it has an aboriginal origin or stake that is even identifiable in less developed economies. I do not presume.

I have done the same, but I was ten years older when I developed the acuity that you have already achieved. I was thirty years older when I had the tools and competence to act upon it. I maintain an interest in you as a cipher or replication of my own story, but with an interesting twist.

There is a paternal cast to my thoughts. Perhaps this very letter could be interpreted as merely the flowering of those thoughts. That would be a simplistic interpretation that would not allow for a further exploration of any possible strategy on my part. While useful when generalizing behavior over small groups or as a shorthand to understanding past actions, the old German psychology serves little useful function when observing an individual. But you already knew that, didn't you?

Paternal may or may not be completely accurate, but I have a larger interest and concern. Your capabilities, the perception that you have trained into yourself, is not the norm. There are few who have the least interest in looking carefully at our world. Of those, most fail to appropriately size themselves within the picture.

Reginald, your work in the last three months has been impressive. I am not surprised that you have chosen now to move on. You may have some secret, internal explanation for leaving. That is good. Blaine reports that you have ineffectually and inconsistently described your reasoning over the last two weeks. That is fine as well. I will tell you that you are leaving because you are now ill-suited to the work and life you currently experience. Your instincts are guiding you elsewhere.

I have not been to Old Charleston, but I know enough about it. I personally think that it is a bad choice for you now. It is easy enough to attribute my opinion the paternalistic tag, and you should ignore my opinion. I understand that my perceptions are both imperfect and imperfectly motivated. I encourage you to embrace it, your time in Old Charleston. I find it ironic that you are guided, perhaps beyond your own keen perception to notice, to mid-sized cities by a trend I triggered twenty years ago.

You could use something bigger, I think. I had hoped you would have made the shorter hop to Portland where I could have introduced you to my friends TJ and Jervis and commended you to a steak at their lovely restaurant. But, I have no say in your peregrinations.

When you are settled, Perhaps you will meet me, perhaps in New York City, for some conversation.

An unusual letter to receive? Unexpected? Difficult to act on? Act upon just this for now:

Reginald, it is not a good time for you to use your silence as a cowl of humility. Be silent but be silent to keep to yourself those thoughts that will disturb your ability to observe. As I understand it, your current production is intent upon asynchronous delivery from your solitude. This cannot last in a healthy life, but right now it is you.

I suspect that you are writing poetry. Do continue. It certainly does not hurt. I hope that the enclosed letter of recommendation has some future value.

With all capable sincerity,

Cardio Plathemy

13

CLEAR *and* SANE

[1983]

IN the year after Cardio met Brady at the car dealership, before Clear and Sane went into effect, Brady had figured out a few things.

Selling cars was not working well when he met Cardio, and it got quite a bit worse. For thirty days he came into the showroom just about every day and encountered people who were interested in buying cars. He knew that they were interested in buying cars because they were uncomfortable and did not want to be on a car lot. Their need for a car forced them to go somewhere unpleasant and speak to someone they did not want to talk to. That someone was Brady, The Car Salesman.

It really got Brady down in the mouth to be so roundly, automatically disliked. He wanted to respond by being as likable as possible, by looking into these people, learning what they needed of him, and becoming that person or thing.

After several unpleasant months, he realized this was not working. Once more standing outside, smoking a cigarette, this time on a very cold January day, he considered his options and decided he was tired, tired of what was essentially a lie. Although he talked to people every day, he missed connecting with people.

The next prospect that came his way was a young couple. He was prematurely bald and she was pregnant. "Hello there," Brady said, "What can I do for you two today?"

"My wife is pregnant and I am going to have to give up my two seat roadster, it looks like."

"I see. Seems a tragedy. How are you doing with letting go of that roadster?" Brady looked over the man's shoulder to the parking lot and spied a red Datsun. "Is that your 1600?"

"Yes, indeed. Her stomach almost touches the jockey box already. I don't have much time to get another vehicle for us."

"I see I see. I must admit that I don't have much interest in children or pregnancy, but it seems that is a pretty serious bind. I can help you check out our cars, but I don't think that you will find anything that has the spirit of your 1600."

The woman had a look of placid consternation. The man was more alight than when he walked in. "I expect not. They do not make them like that anymore."

"How long have you had it?"

"I bought her five years ago, before I met Denise. It is a 1970, the last year of the production line and I had wanted one since I was a kid. Took out a loan and bought it."

"Well I'll be. Looks like you have taken good care of it. I can never take that good care of anything. Why are you at the BMW dealership?"

Denise spoke up. "They are safe, the BMWs."

"Denise wants us to have a safe car, what with all the accidents people are having these days."

This should have been a great opportunity for Brady, but he just refused. He knew that traffic accidents were not in fact increasing. He was not going to feed on her unrealistic fear. "People do say that they feel safer in these Beemers," he said, "but they say the same about those Volvos and Cadillacs."

"We were talking about Volvos!" Denise said. Her look of consternation migrated to her husband's face, "my friend has one and really likes it."

So here they were, at the compromise dealership. Perhaps BMW could offer a car that she felt was safe and he felt had a soul. Brady felt for the couple, changing before his eyes.

"My friend, you should get the Volvo. Your car is just not going to be the source of your sense of manhood anymore. You can look to your children for that, or your job. Spending money right now on the BMW label just so you can think that you are still driving a performance car will take food out of the mouth of your children, tuition out of their college education."

Brady gripped the man's shoulder with the grip of a father speaking to a son. The two men were of about the same age, but Brady reached out with the certainty that came from knowing this was the last act of his car selling career. He was certainly going to lose this customer and his boss was certainly going to fire him for it. He felt great.

"Don't get the compromise car. Then you will both be unhappy every time you get into the car. It will be a source of sadness. Get the car that makes your wife happy, and when you pine for your roadster days, look into her face and be happy for the present." He gave the man's shoulder a good couple of shakes to emphasize this last point. The man's body shook like an al dente noodle.

There was a silence. The shadows of the two men, frozen in this odd position, created bridgework in the entry of the dealership. "The Volvo dealership is just off I-15." He thought that he saw the beginning of a tear in the man's rapidly blinking eye.

There was more silence. Other people in the dealership endeavored to not pay attention. The exception was Brady's boss, who leaned forward from behind his desk at the back of the room. A pencil swished back and forth between the fingers of his right hand.

The woman added to the bridgework by taking her husband's other hand in both of hers. "Honey, are you OK?"

The glut of silence continued. The man tried to turn to his pregnant wife but was not yet done absorbing Brady's message. Brady felt a certainty of action that he had not felt since starting this job. He felt great, just great.

Finally, Denise's husband turned to her. "Yes, I am sorry honey. I am sorry to drag you out here. He is right. Let's go look at the Volvo." Brady released the man's shoulder. They left, and Brady was fired.

Brady did not know that Denise's father was an exceedingly wealthy man. Brady was not in the car with the couple as they drove down Interstate 15 to the Volvo dealership. He was instead getting into his own car and heading home jobless when she turned to her crying husband, and said, "this car means that much to you. I never realized."

He shifted gears, weeping, and then took her hand.

“You must keep it, this car. I can ask my father to pay for the Volvo. Please.”

Brady was not there, but heard an account of this exchange when he spied the man pulling his red Datsun 1600 into the Arctic Circle parking lot two days later. Denise’s husband was sad to hear that Brady had been fired and surmised that the last straw was Brady’s intervention in his relationship. The man, a manager of a group of insurance salesmen for the second largest insurance company in America, hired Brady there in the parking lot.

As he closed the door of his own car and placed a scribbled note of the address of his new job and a bag of fast food on the passenger seat, Brady thought that selling could be the practice of honesty and affinity.

He looked forward to selling insurance, connecting to people’s fears and offering them a service that soothed them. His customers came to trust that he would not offer them something that didn’t make them feel soothed and less fearful.

14

GOING AWAY PARTY

[2010]

"HOW did you build those random cityscapes in the flight attendant training?"

"It's seemingly random, not really random. There is a function in the programming language that makes random. You just type in 'random parens the range of numbers to choose from.' I don't know how it works."

"Maybe it uses something from the system clock. That would not be random, but hard to predict. Have the same outcome for the user."

"What are you two talking about?" Sarah takes her phone away from her ear and turns back to Phil and John.

"Phil was asking me about those cityscapes in the flight attendant training, where the different buildings and stuff were populated on the fly."

"I read or heard an article or had a dream or something that was about how random, truly random, is hard to achieve."

"I guess that makes sense, particularly with the glorified calculators that we use as computers. How do you ask a calculator to choose any old number? It just does not care enough."

"Seems an academic question, if we can create something that we can't predict, we are good. We can stop this conversation, particularly since we are all done with our cigarettes and it is fucking cold out here."

The trio turns back to the bar entry. As Sarah pulls open the door, John has to start yelling halfway through his sentence to overcome the crowd noise, "I guess in military applications or gambling applications you would, you might seek random that would achieve total uncertainty. Maybe you could catch radio signals or..."

The bar had a concrete floor that treasured every sound. In the morning, when the first worker opened the door and walked across the front room, before he starts the jazz mix he likes to work under, the room resonates every step. Even the rattling of his keys comes back to him.

Now, with the room filled with people, no individual sound stands out. A true cacophony. Sarah is awash in it. She tries to think about what to do next. She should collect her drink, on the table next to Reginald. He is seated in a booth listening to Blaine. They both have small glasses in front of them with a finger or two of scotch holding up an ice cube. Her beer has a coaster on top.

The rest of the room is the backs of people, standing on the hard floor or sitting around small tables. Most of The Green Paintbrush staff came down after the beers and sushi that Blaine brought in for Reginald's last day.

Cherry is here. Sarah spies her sitting at the bar between two empty seats. "I am going to go catch up with Cherry," she says to Blaine and Reginald as she picks the coaster off of her glass.

"Do that," Blaine says.

The other two smokers have reclaimed their seats beside Cherry so Sarah stands behind Cherry's stool.

Blaine turns back to Reginald. "Looking forward to the move?"

"It shouldn't be that hard. I've been living in a small apartment. I don't own too many big things. I do get stressed when I think of the small things, the stuff that I think are really important, that become much larger when I think about them."

Blaine's phone vibrates in his pocket while Reginald is speaking. He manages to do no more than to touch it through his pants. "With a family it is a completely different story. My life is about things, so many things. Moving is a project more than an ordeal. The three boxes of sentimental Christmas decorations have to be safely stowed where they will not be crushed or rattle. The kid's bike is put in toward the end because the kid will want it immediately when we arrive. Moving is a lot of things."

"Do they get larger in your head?"

Blaine was thinking that this was a figurative question and metaphors tend to make him uncomfortable, mostly because he does not come up with them himself very well. "I suppose so."

"I mean, the bike, when it is important, when you picture it going into the truck, does it become much larger and start to fill the truck?"

Blaine wants to be helpful, but can't find a way. "No."

"Oh."

Although this is Reginald's party, he is not the center of attention. The Green Paintbrush people enjoy each other's company and have broken off into familiar groups. This is not that different than any other Friday, actually. It is even the same bar that several of them found themselves the previous Friday. That was the night that Blaine and Sarah had locked themselves in the bathroom towards closing. Eventually, everyone else left. Some of them had their tabs applied to Blaine's. He never mentioned it, but the tab was paid.

Tonight, Sarah was pretty sure that she would not kiss Blaine.

Reginald was not there the night Sarah and Blaine locked themselves in the bathroom, nor had he heard any talk of what happened. He had gone back to his house to pack that Friday. He ended up spreading papers around his living room as he went through a box and became intrigued by a collection of old notes he had made.

It is the end of October, 2010. Reginald had found that the content of this box is largely notes he made in 2006. He could only bring himself to call them notes, not poems. They were awful, worse than what he has been writing recently. They were beautiful, almost as informed as what he had been writing recently. He sat on the floor. On the table was a bottle of wine. He rose to refill his glass until the bottle was empty, then descended back into the ever-spreading paper Sargasso.

"It is a map of us, maybe."

"Dreams like spun sugar"

"Edible only in dreams."

"This dream lacked a map."

Lisa would burn her old drafts, but he had to keep this box. She said that the poem is alone and needs no roots and he said that the poem just fell off of the world and left an outline of itself that slowly fades. Then they would kiss, although he does not remember that part very well.

He will be leaving Spokane soon. His resume was welcomed by a company developing industrial software. They have picked up several contracts partnering with the builders of robots that whiz rapidly across the frame of cars, welding and performing other repetitive steps. His job will be to reduce the errors that operators and managers create when they interfere with the systems without a complete understanding of the design.

He interrupts his thinking to acknowledge Cardio's analysis of his new employer. That letter is still on his kitchen table. "Your new employer is plumbing opportunities in industries with negative growth that are seeking ever-more refined efficiencies to stave off the terror of total transformation."

He will be a long ways from Kell and Hack there, in Charleston. He has no one in South Carolina. The questions he will be asked are unpredictable.

When Hack and Jess asked that question back then, he felt stumped, but invigorated. His face hurt as it often did when he woke, particularly after a long couple of days in Boise with Hack and Jess. That question will drift further away now, with nothing to tie it to Reginald.

Packing, ordering and packaging his items. His thousand things made transportable. Some life in all of them. The spoons from a set he and Lisa split up when he moved out. The photo album his father made of his baby pictures and gave to the grown baby. The outmoded clock radio with an analog dial that he had hung in his kitchen to blare morning talk radio. And a box that held only air that represented a question he could not remember.

As he moved the papers about and sipped wine, he sank below grade at the center of the living room carpet. The three solid walls of the room tilted inward at the top. Reginald was in the base of an ancient diving bell. Lowering, lowering, lowering.

Kell has made a trademark of knocking after he has opened Reginald's door and peers with a falsely guilty expression into the living room. Reginald looked up, then looked back down.

"Can I come in?"

"You have." Kell was still shielding most of his body with the door. Cold night air was seeping by him. Reginald was in short sleeves and could feel his arms prick.

"Working?"

"Not sure. I don't think so. Should be packing. Drinking, mostly."

"Oh good." Kell stepped out from behind the door, a bottle of wine in his hand. There was nothing to record in the diving bell. Reginald had no conclusion. He swished the last of the wine in his cup around then poured it in his mouth. Kell walked past him to the kitchen and pulled an opener out of a drawer.

As the walls tilted back to vertical and the floor back to level, Reginald rose and turned towards the back of his friend Kell. He took a step and put one hand around the neck of the empty wine bottle on the kitchen table.

"Has someone ever asked you something that changed your life?" he says.

Kell always stood back on his heels with his knees slightly bent. A curiously springy pose. He lived across the courtyard from Reginald. They were about the same age. Unlike Reginald, Kell had gone to college in Spokane. He stayed after graduating three years ago. He continued working his job cooking breakfast at a local joint popular with students and visitors. He has plans, frequently. They are different every time Kell brings them up.

Kell removed the foil from the top of the bottle of wine. He paused with his thumb and forefinger pinching the torn corner, looked up for a second, swung his vision at Reginald for a second, then returned his eyes to the bottle. "Ridiculous."

"Indulge me until I am gone. What was it?" said Reginald as he stepped forward and allowed his hand to tip and drag the empty bottle off of the table. Walking brought it along with him, once it was free of the tabletop. He headed for the cardboard box at the end of the kitchen, past Kell, that he used for recycling.

"What are you doing in a dump like this with a cock that big?"

"God." Reginald dropped the bottle into the box without bending down. It did not break but made a very loud noise.

"Yessir?" Kell turned with the newly opened bottle slightly tilted, arrested in the air. Since Reginald still had his glass in the other hand, he lifted it to the area of the lip of Kell's bottle. Kell tipped red wine into the glass. He then turned and took down a glass for himself. "I have no idea, buddy. Nothing comes to mind."

They both take drinks from their tumblers of wine.

Kell smacks his lips. "I am off tomorrow if you need help."

“I am not getting a truck until next week. There just is not that much to do.”

“Ah.” Kell leaned against the kitchen counter and turned toward the layer of paper on the living room carpet. He takes a drink. “Your art.”

“I guess.” They both looked at the papers that sat still, in their places. A crown of four papers, two pulled from a legal pad, one unlined smaller heavier paper with the gaudy frills left from a spiral book. One printed on standard A4 paper. Below these four, some stacking and suggestions of the beginnings of attempts to create order.

“Do you have an address in Charleston yet?”

“I do.”

“So you could submit some poems and have a return address for the SASE.”

“I could.” Took a drink.

“But you won’t.”

“Probably not.”

“With the amount of time you spend on this stuff, it seems you could spend an hour here or there putting stamps on envelopes and sending them to some college rag that would publish it.”

Reginald’s head was swimming a bit. There was a persistent twitch in his right bicep. He leaned back against the oven. “I could,” he said again, and took another drink.

15

OFFICE HOURS

[2002]

CARDIO sat at the small desk beheld by photos of other people's children and was certain that he was losing his grip. His grip on the original goal, that goal that becomes The Green Paintbrush. Here he was reviewing a stack of assignments during his office hours. His cell phone off, he folded his long body to allow for the metal filing case at his feet.

As a part time instructor, he was not granted an office of his own. Rather, he had assigned hours at a shared desk. Other instructors had started a playful competition across the wall behind the desk. A series of Post-its at the top read "CUTE-OFF!" in green pen. Below that were babies, grown children, dogs, and cats. Additional Post-its provided captions and speech balloons for these characters.

Cardio remembered when he worked at The Second Largest Insurance Company In America seeing this sort of thing. In 1984 the Supplies Department sanctioned the requisition of Post-its as an SSP (small scale purchase), akin to legal pads and the approved list of pens. As such, departments could purchase and consume a reasonable amount of Post-its without prior approval.

To Cardio, the Post-it was a curiosity. He first beheld one on an expected bundle of papers arriving as usual through the inter-office mail with the usual inter-office mail routing slip. Below the inter-office mail routing slip was a yellow square of paper with "Cardio, as you requested – John" handwritten.

Redundancy pained Cardio. His first meeting with Post-its was not a positive one and the relationship got off to a pretty bad start. He started zeroing-in on them as he walked between meetings, noting the primary uses of the yellow items. Their deployment fell largely into five categories:

1. Restatement of information in a document, then adhered to that document "as per our conversation, note what I highlighted on page 2."
2. Personal address in a situation requiring none "Here you go, Paul! – K"
3. Personal reminder to the authorial individual, often placed in a public location "Get extra napkins at lunch."
4. Public anonymous reminder "Clean up after spills!"
5. Routing information, such as when the secretary brought duplicate documents for everyone in a boardroom. "Cardio" "Carl" "Don."

The last two applications were, Cardio acknowledged, valid. However he questioned whether the entire Post-it supporting systems – manufacture, transportation, marketing, storage – were justified for these use cases. He particularly bristled when he saw the use of a Post-it on a whiteboard, a device specially designed for temporary writing that now held another layer of disposable writing. Cardio had a habit of making a slight popping sound when frustrated by the world, and he would make that sound whenever he saw a Post-it on a white board. If it was circled in marker, he felt a need to look away.

Years later, here in the college office space, Cardio enjoyed this pastiche of loved organisms quite a bit. He had a habit of scanning the collection when he arrived for his office hour to see if a new person or animal had appeared. The cute-off grew crowded and by necessity there was overlap. However, no one covered over more than 8% of a previous entrant. It seemed an unstated rule. They never covered the eyes of another, either.

It was not Cardio's way to reflect on his self. He did not wonder why he had no person or animal to contribute. There was not some longing to become a part of the ongoing, slow visual conversation. He did have a self-reflected thought; he noted that he was not calculating the lost hours of productivity put towards the wall of love but instead appreciating the spontaneous communal effort put forth for the project.

In the metal case at his feet, he kept the class assignments he needed to grade. He pulled one at a time from the front of the case, closed the case, read through and marked up the assignment hunched over the desk, then returned it to the back of the case, still within the larger hanging folder reading "Fall 2002 Mid-term Assignment."

Surprisingly few students had dropped his class by the no-penalty deadline. He had expected that the amount of math would quickly turn away the future English teachers who were seeking a non-math-intensive math credit. He had expected the amount of circuitous social history to bore science majors seeking some GPA padding.

Both categories generally rose to the challenge and were interested in the class discussion. They tended to declare their major as an introduction to their points. Pre-med: "From a biological perspective…" Psychology: "As someone who thinks about individual psychology…" Business: "As I listen to the discussion, I am thinking about the economic implications…"

Cardio had prepared long lectures that out of necessity restated large amounts of the reading, but by the third week he found that he was interrupted early on with questions regarding that day's text which drove the class into lively discussion. He was flummoxed at first, having spent all that time preparing his notes – notes that included shorthand for facial expressions or other indicators of emotional intent. Then he realized that he could change his tack, simply cue the class with questions, and save time on preparation. Time that he could spend on building his new company.

Oh yes, his company. The Green Paintbrush. By the time the class was mid-term his sales team had landed one of the larger wineries, wresting their website away from a Seattle web firm. The winery moved to The Green Paintbrush on the strength of the food and beverage portfolio already developed in the studio. Also, The Green Paintbrush account manager that came calling had been on the football team in high school with four members of the winery staff. Cardio was satisfied. His visual designers were putting together concepts for the client.

He pulled the next class assignment out of his steel case just as his door cracked open. Cherry peeked through and caught Cardio's long body bent in a series of curious angles as he stilled his hand on the steel case and looked under his armpit to make out who was coming through the door.

His smile, normally somewhat awkward, was even more odd when inverted and framed by his elbow.

"Cherry."

"Professor Plathemy."

"What can I do for you?"

16

CHERRY *at* CARDIO OFFICE HOURS

[2002]

CHERRY wedged herself through the door of the tiny academic office. The door did not fully open because another instructor's file box was in the way. She bounced against the door that bounced against the file box, then turned sideways and slipped through. The door swung closed easily.

Cardio's long legs were somewhat wedged under his desk. He swiveled his body as best he could to face her before working to extricate them from their tangle.

"Do you have a minute? More, actually?" Cherry said. She looked to the visitor chair, which contained a stack of CDs in clear sleeves, each that she could see labeled with different handwriting.

"I have many minutes, my dear Cherry. Move those discs onto that desk behind you and please sit down. I am afraid that my roommates are not great citizens of this small nation of ours. I hope that they have housekeepers at home."

Cherry did as Cardio instructed, pulled her heavy shoulder bag over her head, and placed it on top of her feet, leaning against her shins.

Cardio figured out that it was his own box of assignments that obstructed his feet keeping him from turning. He leaned down and moved the box towards the center of the room so that he could pivot to face her.

Neither spoke during this reshuffling time. For some moments after, they continued to not speak. Cherry realized that she initiated the interaction, but had difficulty composing the next thing to say. She manipulated the closures on the top of her bag, a shoulder bag designed for bicycle messengers, and tried to think of a natural way to start. She couldn't exactly remember why she walked into this office, but she thinks that she is in the right place for right now.

"How am I doing in class, Professor?"

"Cherry. You are doing quite well. As the grades go you are certainly on the way to earning an A. In addition I think that your contributions to class discussion, while irregular, have been immensely valuable. At times, I feel that you have kept conversations valid and useful when they were threatened with vile, droll distraction."

"I really can't stand it when egomaniacs drive discussion to their favorite hunting grounds. I feel a need to step in."

"A curious image you have conjured up, of maniacs hunting conversations, and I should probably be more democratic and sympathetic to my other students – they pay just as much as you to listen to me talk – however, yes. I have appreciated your work to return our chats to a productive topic several times."

"Like when Roy wanted to talk about how bad Microsoft Windows is last class. I just can't stand that."

"Again. Roy pays the same as you, but yes. Thank you. I recall feeling the same as you in boardrooms when I worked for corporations."

"It is a class that requires a bit more from us than we are accustomed to, or I would say it requires something different."

"How do you mean?" Cardio was learning that his role was no longer to guide a conversation to the conclusion that he has already come to, but rather to allow the other member of the conversation to make connections, even perhaps to the extent that this person will move the conversation in a different direction – even a different conclusion.

She recognized the steel box Cardio had pushed into the middle of the room and knew that he put the assignments he collected during class into there. "This midterm took me six hours of effort."

"I had expected that it would take three."

"Your estimates are off, but I will tell you why."

"Oh, do."

"Your assignments require actual original thought, the conclusion is not apparent at the outset, nor is the answer clearly true. True without a doubt."

Excellent, he thought. And in his mind he thanked her. "It is a long time since I was in school, but I must say that I should think university should be about just that sort of thing. Are you saying that most of your classes do not require what you call 'original thought?' "

"That is what I am saying, Professor, that you ask for original thought more consistently than other classes." Her voice had the hint of a taunt to it, her careful restatement of his careful restatement of her careful statement.

"Hmm," He smiled and touched his lip and unfolded his legs, "well, perhaps I am in the wrong university, or perhaps there is no university suited to such things. Perhaps my syllabus is a quirky minstrel show and I am distracting you from the opera of higher education. Ah well, what is to be done?" It was not really a question and he continued without pausing, "If it is so difficult and takes so much time, can you tell me why so few have dropped the class? Even Roy – who has as much right to be here as you – continues to come to class and state his point of view."

"I can't say why Roy does anything, nor most other students most all the time. Professor, I don't really understand most people all that well, so I am probably not a good person to ask that question. Perhaps you should put it on your class evaluation at the end of the semester."

"Oh, I did not know that I had the opportunity to ask for feedback from the students. I will keep that in mind. Sounds like a manner of data collection which would provide a lot of ignorable data points, but perhaps a few gems." Cardio always came off with elitist airs, but when he spoke directly with Cherry he enjoyed her reaction and it encouraged him to act all the more superior.

For as long as they knew each other, this conversation would continue, he giving her the right to feel among an elite and he savoring her joy in that state. In truth, there was no elite to which Cherry truly belonged, but in conversation with Cardio Plathemy she had a sense that there were others around them, and they were equals, and they would understand her.

"Well, I take it you are enjoying the class enough, Cherry."

"Should classes be something that one enjoys?" Her eyes flitted past him to the Cute Off. She had seen it in her previous visits. What a curious use of time and resources, she thought.

"I suppose there are other criteria. Certainly when I set out to teach this class I had different expectations what a person a few short years from educational independence would use to evaluate their life choices. I had a profile of my expected student. It was based on very little information, just a predictive model really." he smiled and touched his lips again, "But... I hear students, both talking to me and overheard when I lunch on campus, and their decisions really do seem to be about fun and only fun. Enjoyment is the dominant decision-making criteria, wouldn't you say?"

"I would, for most."

"Do you enjoy the class?"

She smiled, touched her own lip with a single finger, "I do." Cardio touches his lips with two fingers when he thinks.

"Good. I am glad that you are experiencing what typical students desire here at the university. I am doing my job of providing enjoyment." They both smiled.

"Professor, I really enjoy your class but I see that you are not teaching anything else here."

"Correct. This is the only class that I teach."

"Why do you teach it?"

He paused and considers his answer, breaking the tempo of their usual easy conversation. "I suppose that I felt that such a course needed to exist." It was a lie and he felt inside of him a slight churning as he lied to Cherry.

"You are a paladin of critical thinking, then? A pioneer of interdisciplinary courseware? Is that it?" The same teasing tone, "What else do you do with your time?"

He smiled again. "I am retired, as you know, from a job at an insurance company. I teach, I catch up on my reading, and I run a small local company that designs web pages."

Cherry forced a twinkle into her eye and gripped the top handle of her messenger bag at the same time. "I see. So you don't financially need to teach to make ends meet? Most of my professors are not financially independent, you know. Those without tenure are aware that student evaluations can determine whether they get a new contract. Those teaching part time are seeking more classes to teach. Surely when you meet with them you notice that there is some difference between you and them."

Cardio adopted a conspiratorial tone with Cherry, "I must confess that I do not find much time to meet with them. I generally have an important conflict when there are department meetings, and social events for faculty serve no function for me."

He became aware of a sense of playfulness in himself that he normally feels only in isolation, when contorting data. Sharing a playful moment with another, another with motives, invites a certainty of chaos that he would normally avoid. Perhaps, if The Green Paintbrush is to succeed, this is an experience to which he must become accustomed.

"I see, Professor Plathemy."

"I do believe that you do."

"So, why do you teach this course at all?"

"You have already asked me that and I see no reason to change my answer." A very good try, he thinks. And he is intrigued to find out what she is getting at.

"I see. Or rather I don't but I know a brick wall when I see it."

"Perhaps there is a door in that wall somewhere."

"How is your web designing going?"

"Well, quite promising. We are going to be making a site for a local winery. Quite high profile. Our biggest client yet!"

"Why did you start a company to design web pages? You don't actually design web pages yourself."

"No, I don't."

"Another wall."

A smile. "You seem rather computer savvy. Have you ever designed a web page?"

"A little."

"It is a brave new world, it seems. Such a new career. My web designers have any number of degrees and backgrounds. One is actually a certified farrier. That means he can shoe horses!"

They both laugh in a somewhat staged manner, then he continues, "I wonder if you have an aptitude for it. Do you (he emphasizes the word with an expert tone) *enjoy* designing web pages and programming computers?"

"I do."

“Cherry, I hate to ask, but perhaps you could help me. This new site, the one for the winery, is a big job and no one on my staff is ready for it. I wonder if you could be just the person to help us. I wonder, and I hate to ask you to divert your attention from your academic career, here in a place rife with so much enjoyment, but would you come in to The Green Paintbrush office and we could talk about what your experience is, your capabilities, your availability...”

Cherry released her grip on the messenger bag and stopped smiling. She leaned back and then leaned forward, and then leaned back again. “I guess that I could meet, sure. When are you in the office there?”

“Oh let’s see.” He tries to be serious but overacts, looking up and tapping his two fingers again across his lips. “When are you out of class tomorrow?”

“My last class is over at 10:50.”

“Could you be downtown by 1?”

“Yes.”

Cardio turned back to the desk. He took up the Post-it pad and a green pen. He wrote the address of The Green Paintbrush, then paused and turned to look at her. Cherry was turning red at the edges of her face, at her scalp. It stood out against her hair. Her mouth was slightly open but she busied herself opening her bag. She then put her hand against two objects inside, and then closed it again.

Cardio turned back to the Post-it and bent over it, pen again against the tiny paper. He peeled it off of the pad and started to hand it to her. He felt elation, triumph, worry. “Here is the office address. Oh. Wait.” He pulled the Post-it back from her outstretched hand and turned once again to the desk. She dropped her hand as he once again leaned over the desk. His feet twisted and kicked a little while he concentrated.

“Here.” The Post-it had been folded into a boat, then stuck to the outstretched hand of a two year old that Cardio had pulled from the Cute Off wall.

“What shall I bring?”

“A resume. And bring that first assignment for class. And bring links to websites that you like and do not like.”

“How many?”

“As many as you need to make the point, Cherry.”

Cardio did not actually need her to bring anything. He had used a website called Google to search for mentions of her unique name and had found web pages she had written for family member's businesses, for some political activists, and an odd experiment in linking public art installations to public tragedies. He knew what Cherry was capable of making.

She did not know that Cardio was aware that Cherry was under academic probation and would most certainly lose her financial aid after this term. It was months later that she realized that he knew why she had come to his office that day, even though in the course of their conversation she never managed to say what she had intended to, which was goodbye.

She opened the door as far as it would, turned sideways and exited. Her shoulder bag was not over her neck but simply off one shoulder, an awkward position best only for hurried exits. Her opposite hand cradled the small boy that held the boat that held the address. Only when she got back to her room did she unfold the boat and find that, underneath the address of The Green Paintbrush – data she already knew–Cardio had hastily drawn a door.

17

REGINALD *and the* QUESTION

[2010]

REGINALD could not figure where to put the nearly empty box, the box that contained air and a question he could not recall.

He had originally planned for it to ride deep in the truck, safely stowed for the trip. That it would sleep all the way to Charleston and when he arrived it would stretch its arms out of the box into the southern sun and shout out itself.

But then he considered that the question could ride alongside him on the passenger seat. He could silently consider it in different contexts, starting with a path through Boise. He would add a full day to take the southern route and pass through Boise. Where is the box most like text on a white screen? When it does not interact and is not touchable or when it is before you, changing its context with every mile.

It did not occur to Reginald that he could try one approach for part of the trip and then try another approach for the other. This is somewhat understandable in that the placement of a largely empty box is clearly symbolic, an obscure character stamped onto a piece of paper. As such, the meaning, usage, and power of the box was entirely up to the author, the one who stamped that letter onto that paper. As he contemplated the box, he felt that it could not change positions throughout the trip. It needed to be in the cab or in the back of the truck. One or the other.

On a call with his father over the weekend, they talked about the relative merits of taking Reginald's not-very-nice furniture across country versus buying new humdrum furniture when he arrived.

His father liked toying with ideas like this, "Well, take into account the cost of gas to move all of that weight. That is not insignificant."

"True. And all the time loading and unloading."

"On the other hand, you will have a lot to do when you reach Charleston. Furniture shopping would be quite a chore!"

"True." Reginald was staring at a leg and thigh of chicken, sitting on a plate on his kitchen counter. Steam rose from it. It smelled delicious. He pinched off a piece of skin and sucked on it as silently as possible.

"Have you decided what route to take?"

"I am going to go south. I figured it would be less trouble this time of year." This is true, but he also thought that taking the empty box through Boise would trigger something inside, that a genie could coalesce in the cab of his truck and tell him what the question had been.

"Well, we don't have any family or friends that I can recall that-a-way. Your aunt will be sorry to miss you, but I understand. Makes sense. No problem," his dad said. A dog barked through the phone.

His father does not have a cell phone. He held a cordless phone to his ear while leaning in a hallway next to his back door. The phone base unit is mounted to the wall next to where he leans. Although his house has had a wireless phone for many years, Reginald's father seems to not yet have accepted the fact that he is not tied to the phone base with a long, snaking cord. Reginald thinks that his father may be trying to be nice to the phone by asking it to transmit over shorter distances.

"Hey dad, my dinner is getting cold. I need to go."

"Oh yeah, OK. Love you, Reginald. Let me know what you decide about the furniture. I am curious."

"Sure. Love you."

Reginald put his cell phone down next to the plate and picked up the chicken leg. He bent one leg and leaned over the kitchen counter. Before him was everything he owned. On the carpeted floor, where he had spread loose paper when trying to pack a few days ago, was an apparently chaotic amalgam of boxes and dismembered furniture.

An order would become apparent if you observe it more carefully. Nearer to the door, he had large boxes and regularly shaped items, such as his night stand. Nearer where he stood in the kitchen the items descended into a chaos of chairs, lamps, and other awkward shapes. To complete the visual experience, he had capriciously made the first two stacks near the entrance extremely ordered. He had applied a straight edge to the stack after first selecting boxes that tapered pleasantly. No box was wider in any dimension than the one below it.

In the next section he twisted the stacks slightly and deliberately included one box that was slightly narrower and slightly longer than the box below it.

He panned to the final section, containing the lamps and chairs. He had nested the smaller boxes amongst the awkward objects, deliberately perching them at odd angles, as though they were falling or spinning through space.

Spinning through space. Debris. Reginald chewed chicken, somewhat open mouthed. He did not have a napkin and rubbed the chicken grease onto the back of his forearm after every couple of bites.

He could not quite remember why he was moving. His phone briefly created the noise of a belt sander starting up, vibrating against the table. He spread his hand and rubbed it thoroughly up and down his pant leg a couple of times then flipped his phone over.

In the neighborhood. Can I drop by?

His phone labeled incoming messages with a picture and the first part of that person's most recent social media post. Cherry's most recent Twitter post was, "Looking forward to the SXSW schedule released next..."

Reginald had put his hand back on his chicken while reading the short message. To reply he first stuck his greasy index finger into his mouth then flicked it back and forth on the front of his shirt to dry it.

Sure, come in.doors open.

She responded quite quickly.

They do.

It is not often that Reginald slipped up grammatically or made typos, so Cherry must have been pretty satisfied to mock his failure to type "door's" or "door is." She must have also been very close by. The door opened before Reginald could think of a comeback.

18

CHERRY STARTS

[2010]

CHERRY is outside of Reginald's apartment complex. She is gripping her phone in the pocket of her light coat. It is late afternoon and the light of the sun is a frank voice. It draws boundaries between buildings and ground and it ticks off time.

Her phone has betrayed her and has texted Reginald and now she is moving quickly to his door. The faster she moves the less time for either of them to prepare. She comes through the door.

"Well I will be damned," she says, "doors do open."

"And close, too," Reginald says. He is holding his left greasy hand with the fingers splayed. Cherry notices that this is a pointless but common manner, as if the greasiness must not cross from finger to finger. One could hold a greasy or dirty hand the same way one holds a clean hand, but no one does. It provides a visual cue to those around you. Perhaps she could train herself to control that habit; perhaps she could actually project that sense of dirtiness at any moment. That would be interesting. She cannot think of a use case, but keeps the thought alive.

Reginald sees her sprouts of dyed blonde hair with the self conscious roots, her unzipped hooded sweatshirt with the weight of her large cell phone in the left pocket dragging it down below her waist on one side. Reginald notices that he tends to stop noting elements of people around the waist and yet the fashion shoe industry is giant and many people have an urgency to own appropriate shoes. He must be missing something, or else it is a market that was fabricated. It would be hard to develop a certainty about that.

He does not want to turn his back on her but needs to wash his hands. He needs to say something as he is turning to acknowledge her and simultaneously take care of his uncomfortable chicken grease hand. He can't think of anything and stands there with one hand splayed in the air.

There is no place to sit or even head towards – except to Reginald. Cherry is in a hallway of his boxes and she could only step towards him, stand still, or leave. She has closed the door and now stands just to the side of it, her shoulder near to the neatest stack in the room.

From a top view, this room has a great deal of interesting elements. They suggest a scalar relationship between two categories: Reginald's packing and the people who occupy the room. Say the chaos-to-order exhibit that Reginald has made moves from left to right, then Reginald is just beyond the most extremely chaotic point and Cherry stands at the point of greatest order.

"Come in. Come farther in, Cherry. Sorry I don't think I have anything comfortable to sit on. Want to lean on my counter and have a glass of wine?" He does not want to turn from her, wants her to feel as welcome as he can manage, so his hand stays greasy.

Cherry surveys the boxes and steps forward. "Sure." She touches the first slightly twisted stack and then her eyes pan to a chaotic tripod of items: four legs of a table taped together, a curtain rod, and a camera tripod. She smiles.

"Great. Let me open a bottle. Make yourself as at home as possible here in this madness." He is glad to have permission and a reason to turn. And glad that he has a bottle of wine in the house. He grabs a dishcloth and wipes his hand down, then flops the cloth onto the counter. They are both moving simultaneously, she to the gap in the kitchen counter, the passageway to the apartment kitchen, and he deeper into the kitchen to retrieve a bottle and a corkscrew.

"The chaos of it all," Cherry says.

"What? Yes," says Reginald, interrupted reaching for the bottle, turning to her empty handed, realizing that she is talking about the packed life before her, and turning back to retrieve the wine. "Packing is interesting. Moving is interesting. All these objects, taken into account, as a whole are your life, as a collection are just an ordering problem, as individual items are connected to memories and plans and all these abstractions."

"You have a good mind, you bastard."

Reginald wills himself to not pause as he levers the cork out of the bottle, "Thank you I guess." Then he puts his hands to his side, holding the corkscrew, the cork still impaled.

"I did not want it because it always destroys beautiful things, beautiful moments, beautiful interactions. Because I wanted to keep engaging with you the way we were, I did not want it." She took up the bottle and poured two glasses. "I don't want to feel as horrible as I do. I don't want to be as angry as I am. It is beyond my control, it is an entity of itself.

"I thought at first that I had to stop it, but now I believe that it has a right to exist as well, this entity of feeling. I listen to it. It feels horrible to carry this around, but I have to."

She takes a sip. He has reached his hand around his glass but has not lifted it from the counter. "It fucking hates you. I hate you for bringing this to me. I hate you for being a fucking asshole. I hate you for ruining what was beautiful."

She takes another drink. Reginald drinks cheap, uninteresting wine. "I did not know any of this until I started talking just now, not really. Not in the way that I do now that I have verbalized it. This has all been entirely unrecorded until this moment."

Reginald knows that this moment will feel important for a long time. He wonders, when he packs it away after she leaves, where in the scale of order to chaos it should be placed. "I am glad you came here today and talked to me. I have missed talking to you." He says this instead of saying "I'm sorry" because saying "I'm sorry" sounded so insincere when he said it in his head. Now, saying "I have missed talking to you" sounds like he is changing the subject or not properly sympathetic. He thinks he should not try to be properly sympathetic because there is no possible way to sound properly sympathetic. All in all, Reginald feels pretty bad. He takes a drink of wine, which does not seem like the right thing to do either.

"I am very very sorry," he says. It sounds as empty as he thought it would.

They are drinking from cheap glass tumblers, bought from a supermarket in a set of six. They are thin walled and thin based, pretty lightweight. Cherry takes one good drink and, instead of lowering the glass to the counter, flings it into the midst of the stacked boxes. It bounces and splashes across cardboard then falls to the carpet, miraculously unbroken.

They look at each other. Reginald will accept any word, any action. He is ready – not for anything – he is ready for nothing. He takes his hands off the counter, stands up feeling like leaning on the counter is too casual a pose. His hands hang at his side, which feels awkward which he thinks what he should feel is awkward.

Cherry's face is full of life. Her shoulders are back, a redness to her skin at the border of her scalp. Her mouth is slightly open. "Sorry." Cherry looks down at the Formica countertop. "Fuck. Did I just say to you that I am sorry? Fuck." She walks to the door, head down. She walks through the door and closes it. She pulls it carefully to make sure it latches.

19

BRADY, CLEAR *and* SANE

[1984]

BRADY kept a much neater office than was necessary, and it required some effort. The amount of paper that a busy insurance agent had to move around invited clutter, but Brady took the time to sort and dispense files. Even at the end of a day, he would take an extra ten minutes before he went out the door to put the last case folders away in the appropriate cabinet, or into the hopper destined for a runner to deliver back to the main repository.

The runners probably never noticed that he alphabetized the outgoing case folders.

Other agents would teasingly note Brady's cleanliness and attempt to come up with nicknames associated with this attribute. However, insurance agents are not a generally creative group. Tidy Brady was the best they could summon.

To Brady, it was not neatness, but completeness. His job was not done until the paper had made the trip back to the central repository and although he was not responsible for the entire ecosystem of that paper, he wanted to do all that he could to move the process along.

Agents who had been in the office for years, unlike Brady, felt the significant increase in paperwork with the new protocols instituted at the Second Largest Insurance Company in America. Brady's hiring coincided with the new practices, so he did not feel the pain of adaptation that the more experienced agents felt. None of them, including Brady, realized that Brady was the inspiration for the new protocols. Nor did Brady fully realize the losses that other agents were feeling due to the new rules at The Second Largest Insurance Company in America.

The requirement was easy to state but became something of a bear to institute. New applications for car insurance had to be accompanied by an essay of at least 300 words titled "Why I Drive." This essay, or if it was long simply selected portions, was to be read aloud to the insurance agent upon signing the insurance agreement.

It was somewhat controversial and garnered press coverage. The press sometimes took a playful tone with this innovative approach to insuring motor vehicles. Sometimes, reporters and commentators were quite hostile, citing issues of literacy, disability, and language. As a result, The Second Largest Insurance Company had to establish processes for deaf and mute people. Brady had to learn these but was never called upon to apply them; never had any deaf drivers come to him for insurance. After a lawsuit was threatened, The Second Largest Insurance Company established processes to use translators for people who spoke other languages, which gave Brady the chance to occasionally work with very interesting people from Vietnam and Mexico.

Often, the Vietnamese would bring an English-speaking family member with them. For the purposes of conversation, this usually functioned just fine. However, Cardio's directives were quite clear about the essay; it must be penned and spoken by the client alone. As such, Brady would call in a translator hired by his company to make sure the friendly translator was not aiding the essay along.

His smallish office would sometimes be a little cramped when two clients, himself, and a translator all gathered for an essay reading. It felt like quite a ceremony sometimes.

He liked how the four of them would sit. Behind a desk, Brady occupied a large portion of the room. Directly before him was an open space. Beyond that, the door to one side and the clients to the other. This day, the driver was a smaller Vietnamese man perhaps in his fifties. He had scooted his heavy chair so that it touched his young son's. They both wore very white, buttoned shirts.

To one side, the Vietnamese translator Maiv-Tshua sat in a light, armless chair just a few centimeters off of the wall. While the chair was neutrally pointed to the open space between the client and Brady's desk, she tilted herself towards the door and the client. She kept her hands in her lap except to occasionally swipe a strand of hair back behind her ear. She always wore a pantsuit when called upon to meet with Brady and a client.

Brady always dressed carefully for work, and noted that the four of them were quite a well-groomed quartet. Brady never discerned any meaning in the foreign language but instead heard it as music and the English translation as a counterpoint.

(Musical line)

(counterpoint) "I drive to get to work at the airport and sometimes I drive to take my wife to the store to buy groceries."

Brady nods at the man, then nods at Maiv-Tshua.

(Musical line)

(counterpoint) "The drive to the airport is easy at four in the morning. Few others are on the road. I turn the lights on and then after I have pulled away from the house I turn on the radio."

The man smiled a little during the next (Musical line). Maiv-Tshua paused and covered her mouth for a second before she starts in. The man's son laughed aloud.

"I listen to the radio to hear more English, but for the first week I took that drive I did not know that I was listening to a station for Mexicans. It was not English at all!"

Brady laughed aloud, relieved to be able to share the joke. Everyone's smiles and laughter joined together in the small room for a time. Brady did not think about the geometry of the people in the room, nor the function of essays in creating better drivers. He thought that he loved this workday that had discovered him in the parking lot of an Arctic Circle restaurant.

20

DON SWEATING *the* DETAILS

[1984]

THE press, and just about every third person that read their essay to Brady, felt it necessary to make jokes about grades. The Second Largest Insurance Company was not giving out grades. It was not necessary to say anything in particular in the essay, it merely had to exist. Every year, to renew your insurance, you had to return to your agent and read him a new essay.

Spot checking was done at central repositories to confirm that family members or other people with known relationships did not turn in identical essays, but Cardio had instructed the organization to not spend its usual massive effort on reducing fraud. It took some time for the processors and their overseers to understand that the critical part of the whole process was the client reading their essay aloud.

At the outset, Cardio had emphasized to Don and then to the CEO that there would be a dip in business. Don, still a vice president, was aware that his competitors were stoking the fires of public opinion with advertisements mocking his new protocol. They would look at each other in meetings, Don and Cardio. Don would be excited and nervous, drawing triangles on his legal pad. He would look up at Cardio, who would raise both eyebrows nearly imperceptibly and then turn away. Don was always calmed by that action.

"The provided discount clearly not offsetting the loss from hesitant buyers..."

“In certain regions, statistics are suggesting cultural pressure against.”

“Joke on Johnny Carson last week.”

Don loved Johnny Carson. When Johnny did a bit mocking a customer of the Second Largest Insurance Company in America for having stage fright while reading his essay aloud, Don’s feelings were extremely mixed. He got up from his couch and found his briefcase, wherein he kept a copy of Cardio’s internal-only briefing document. The document was one paragraph with four footnotes and then a long line chart covering five years.

He put his finger on the dip in sales, then on the following dip in claims-to-accounts ratio.

As the claims ratio decreases, we can continue to lower rates, even for existing customers. The novelty of the essays will expire in nine to eighteen months at which time we will have the first batch of supporting data...

Don was not sure if Johnny was mocking him personally. If so – if Johnny Carson was making fun of Don – then what good would it be for him to become CEO? He needed to believe in this data.

Perhaps this data could elicit an amazing turn around in Johnny’s position. Perhaps, if this was all true, this line chart could propel him into the chair next to Johnny. Yes, perhaps someday these essays could become a permanent part of America, forever associated with The Second Largest Insurance Company in America and with their new CEO. He could be invited to Carson and tell tales of funny essays that they received and close with a touching statement about how accident rates have dropped and that is what really matters. Then a joke about a monkey driving a car and they go to commercial.

This might yet work out just fine. He just needs to hold the line, keep the faith. Don put the briefing back into his briefcase and went to bed.

21

CHERRY *at the* GREEN PAINTBRUSH

[2003]

BLAINE, Cardio, and Cherry stood around Cardio's custom conference table in the offices of The Green Paintbrush.

"I thought there would be a closed door," said Cherry.

She grasped both hands at the edge of the large, circular glass-topped table. It sat just apart from a bank of desks. The designers at those desks continued staring at their screens, which flickered with their efforts.

Cherry can make people nervous. Her large eyes are easy to track. They wander a room, and then fixate on something over your shoulder. While you are talking to her, her eyes will scan you and the space behind you. She might raise both eyebrows slightly while staring over your shoulder, hopefully not in relation to anything you are saying.

Twice during their short meeting Blaine broke up the conversation by turning around to try to understand what drove her expression.

Cardio, standing beside him, jumped in the second time with a follow up question. "So in this example, what is the major problem that you see?"

Cherry tilted the top of the piece of paper in front of her upward by pinching it between her thumb and a small platform made by her first two fingers. "The links at the top and the links at the left are totally redundant, Professor." Blaine smiled and whipped his head from Cherry's invisible location to look at Professor Plathemy. "And yet worded differently, so if

I have a desire to see everything on the site, I will click through and be disappointed that I am at a place I have already visited. Disappointed and a little disoriented, I think."

Blaine looked at the page between him and Cardio, a duplicate of what Cherry held. "This is the standard C-clamp navigation that is used by modern websites, you know."

"I do see it around a lot. I am not sure that the visual form is the problem. I think the text in this example is just poor. Although, this C-clamp does seem to allow the designer to lose control of the viewer pretty quickly. So many options."

Before Blaine could respond, Cardio slid the paper to his opposite side, away from Blaine and off of the stage. "Show us something that you do like."

Cherry dropped below the surface of the table to where she had left her messenger bag. She held the handle in her hands, knees bent and flipped open the bag with an expert exertion.

After grabbing the next manila folder, she turned and looked up. Through the glass she made eye contact with Blaine. Cardio lowered his eyes and also looked at her through the glass.

She quickly rose above the surface and took in a big breath. Blaine had not seen a designer that used manila folders before. In fact, Blaine was not exactly sure that she was in fact a designer. She was awkward enough, but not in the way that he was used to in designers.

"This site has limited navigation but a dominant search bar. I like that. I think that with a lot of pages, I would rather not click five times and instead type a word or two and look for results."

"But then the designer has completely lost control," said Blaine, "like you said about the C-clamp.

"Well," Cherry's eyes swirled around the room for a second. Her hands swept out, then back to center across the tabletop, "This site does something different. It wants you to find value in the very site, not in the product it sells." She seemed pretty proud of this statement.

"What is the difference to the website owner, Cherry?" Cardio took the sample from her hands and spun it on the table to face him. Blaine tilted his head unnecessarily and looked at the page.

"Both want the viewer to leave with a good feeling," Cherry said. Blaine believed that she was making this up as she went along, "but this one with the search bar wants a longer term relationship with the viewer. They want them to return. The owners of the other site seems to want me to dial their phone number then close the browser window forever."

"I think you are making that answer up," said Cardio, "but it is a reasonable answer. Also, it opens up a number of interesting questions. In that context, is the first website all that bad? Does it succeed in getting you to want to dial that number?"

Cherry paused for an unnaturally long time. "I think they seem less than thoughtful and they alienated me. I don't believe that conversation would start off on the right foot." Blaine thought that the pause was very un-designer-like.

Blaine wanted to check his phone. Instead he sorted the two pieces of paper in front of him. He felt that he should be paying more attention than he could bring himself to, since it seemed apparent that Cardio was going to hire this girl and Blaine would need to understand her well enough to be in the office with her and ask her to do things. Knowing that his genial face would not project his disinterest, he allowed his mind to roam while maintaining an expression of complete engagement. It seemed time to say something. They were nearing the end of the appointment.

"Very good, Cherry. Can you tell us what your salary requirements are?"

Cardio flicked his eyebrows, "That is, if you are prepared to at this point, Cherry." He did not return Blaine's quick look in his direction.

Cherry did not say anything for a good long while. Her eyes strayed to multiple points in the room, drawing her face in multiple directions. She needed enough to live on, whatever that was. "How much does the job pay?"

Blaine started to say what he was supposed to say, "salary is based upon experience and applicable..." before he was interrupted by Cardio, "You get paid either what you are worth, or the value that the market assigns to you, whichever comes out first, my dear."

Blaine's face dwelt on Cardio's profile for long enough to transmit three confusing concerns: the interruption of his human resources legally defensible phrasing, the opening for a budget-busting salary negotiation with a junior, and the use of the term "my dear" in a job interview. Cardio still did not turn or even flick his eyes towards Blaine. Instead he looked demurely at the candidate and then down at his incomprehensible notes. Blaine looked down and saw the word "Potentate of Process" circled.

Blaine missed Seattle sometimes. He missed San Francisco more than he would like to admit.

It is easy enough for Blaine to wrap up such a meeting, including the awkward moments of offering a hand to shake to a girl who avoids eye contact and moving her towards the door.

Blaine could have asked Cardio about Cherry and perhaps even used some energy to express some anger or discomfort that Cardio would disrupt Blaine's interviewing habits. However, he had thus far found Cardio's ways impenetrable. One of Blaine's great abilities was to allow concerns or unsolvable issues to drain quickly through the floor of his thoughts. This was a great benefit when working for Cardio in Spokane, as there were few if any organizations here that cared for Blaine's skills in this area. If for some reason an ill-posed question disrupted his work, he may have to move his family yet again.

22

CLEAR *and* SANE *in* PRACTICE *and* EFFECT

[1985]

IT is said that people do not like change. This is not entirely true. People do not like the moment before change, when they are considering outcomes. When it comes to public policy, good dictators know to give people as little time to think about change as possible. Do not pause and ask for input. Put on the crown, disperse the crowds with tear gas, and start the regime.

These two parallel changes in American driving culture, the Second Largest Insurance Company in America Why I Drive Essay Program and Clear and Sane Roads, are a matched pair of case studies on instituting change.

Clear and Sane was instituted by a public body in a nation with gargantuan industries whose sole production is words and pictures. These industries package their words and pictures in magazines, television shows, and morning radio commentary. In order to provide the audience with predictability, the media companies commit to providing a package of words and pictures of a regular size on a regular basis. If an audience member subscribes to TIME Magazine, the publishers of TIME Magazine commit to delivering a same-sized package of words and pictures at the same time every month.

Cardio reflected on this one day in his car on the way back to his office. He had just come from an appointment with his dentist wherein he had scanned a TIME Magazine during the 14 minutes he was waiting prior to his scheduled teeth cleaning. Clear and Sane had been passed two months before and was four months from implementation. TIME had a matched pair of articles on Clear and Sane. One an authoritative analysis of predicted outcomes, the other a more personal story about a rural police force preparing for the changes to come. TIME likes that change is on the horizon, thought Cardio. Gives them something to fill the page.

He could not calculate the exact media response when The Second Largest Insurance Company started asking for an essay from every driver. He hoped that it would be a short cycle of impact stories, which would be something of an advertising boon, but not any long-term themes or recurring jokes across media and water coolers. That would give individuals too much material for thought at the moment before change.

Unlike the federal government, Cardio could act like a despot. Once the internal organs of The Second Largest Insurance Company in America decided on Cardio's plan, they simply enacted the policy. Individuals had to respond to it by either writing an essay or contacting a welcoming sales person at The First Largest Insurance Company in America to jump ship.

The dentist had given him a clean bill of health, which Cardio expected. He had calculated that following a schedule of brushing and flossing was overall less time and resources than having deep cleanings and the statistical probability of cavities. This calculation had included the cost of toothpaste. He examined whether the ingredients of toothpaste were subject to market variations that may alter that cost above a certain threshold. He found that competitive pressures balanced out any concerns with that. Toothpaste cost was not highly flexible.

The first essays were coming in from pilot programs and into the processing centers. Cardio was wondering if there was data available that would allow one to measure the impact of good dental health on lifespan, correcting for other correlated factors such as good general health and education. He should look into that, he thought.

23

REGINALD CROSSES AMERICA

[2010]

THE truck had cruise control, which Reginald was thankful for. It allowed him to comfortably travel at a slightly higher rate. It was overall much less stressful than controlling speed himself. However, on a long downhill he noticed that the cruise control allowed the truck to speed up to 104 kilometers per hour and he had to apply the brake. Some modern cars had alarms which beeped slightly when the vehicle achieved common speed limits such as 50, 80, and 100. This rented truck did not have that feature.

Reginald had rarely driven for the previous year. His small Spokane world was easy to navigate by bicycle. Today he had found the road relaxing, a space to breathe and experiment with harmonizing with the various sounds of the truck: engine noise, wheels on road, wind buffeting windshield.

Long before he got to Boise he had stopped thinking about the box at all. It had fallen from the seat and was on the floorboards. As he drove through the sunny plains he took off his jacket. When he had tossed it across the bench seat it covered the small box.

At the first Boise mileage sign Reginald self-consciously pulled his jacket off of the box. It was on its side still, on the floorboards when he drove through Boise. When he pondered pulling into the city – he got in to the right lane preparing to exit the freeway – it seemed to jiggle slightly.

He felt that nothing would happen in Boise to change the pitch or direction of his journey. With a large truck and a bit of a feeling of urgency, he decided to skip Boise and push on to Salt Lake City, a natural place to stay the night before giving up Interstate 84 for Interstate 80. I-80, which he would take all the way to Lincoln, Nebraska.

He changed lanes back to the left and continued on. He was surprised to hear a honking horn. In the short time that he had been in the right lane a car had moved up into his blind spot. Reginald felt a short rush of energy when the horn sounded. He swung the wheel too hard back into the right lane. Had Reginald slowed down? No, the cruise control was still set to 97. The other driver must have been speeding to come alongside him so quickly.

The car backed off and flashed his lights to let Reginald in, perhaps hoping that some act of consilience would earn him forgiveness. It was not to be.

At the next onramp a police motorcycle swept behind the car and turned on his lights. Reginald watched in his side view mirror as the car pulled over. Reginald projected a crestfallen expression onto the little silhouette of the driver in his mirror as he slowed to accept his expensive fate.

In the desert dusk, Reginald pulled the truck into the parking lot of a Super 8 Motel in Salt Lake City and checked in. He did not go straight to his room but jogged across the street to an Arctic Circle restaurant to grab some takeout before they closed.

Carrying the familiar fast food bag, Reginald paused briefly at the glass door of the restaurant. This freeway-side oasis of hotels and restaurants. Each lot sporting carefully sculpted lawns, rock walkways, and low hedges that define their territory. The vast un-managed space around persisted as desert. Dirt, low plants of tan and pale green, rocks, dried out remains of scrubby trees.

In between the two worlds, set off by the flat, powerful blue of the gloaming sky, was a plastic chicken standing guard over the entrance to the Arctic Circle drive through. Reginald jogged his food back to the truck, fished through his coat pocket for a small digital camera. Leaving his dinner in the cab of the truck, he jogged back across the street to the chicken. First he took a picture from the spot that he first spied the scene. He was careful to get all the elements: lawn, chicken, desert, sky. Not a very experienced photographer, he was unsure that the lens and two megapixel file size would properly render the information. He crouched at the foot of the chicken and took a picture of simply those two elements: chicken, sky.

Returning to the truck, he opened the door and said aloud, "remember to keep the camera with you." He collected his food, a small shoulder bag, his jacket, and the box with a question within.

In his room, he ate a burger and wrote at the desk. Reginald chewed and looked out the window at his rented truck and beyond it a freeway. His mind could still see a speedometer locked at 97 kilometers per hour when he relaxed his perception.

Reginald was pretty certain that the driver of that car, a faceless and genderless individual to him, was going to be unable to drive for 30 days, the usual cost of a speeding infraction. It seemed rather a light sentence to Reginald, considering how disturbing that moment was, how ten minutes later he realized his jaw was clenched and the spontaneous sweat that had erupted from his skin was evaporating and chilling his arms. He had smelled the sweat in the small cab of the truck and rolled the window down.

24

CARDIO LEAVES

[2005]

"CHERRY, have you some time for me today?" Cardio put one finger on the desk next to Cherry without bending down. She swished her head in his direction and back to the computer screen.

"Checking. I think so. Sure." Boxes were shrinking and growing on her screen as she turned her attention to her online calendar. "When, more specifically, were you thinking?"

"I would be anxious to sit with you as soon as possible. Actually, as I think of it, perhaps we could take a short walk."

Cherry scrunched her face for a second and jerked her neck backwards. "um, how long will that take?"

"I see over your shoulder that right now and until eleven you are committed to single tasking on the personal network design project. That is important but not impending. Could we go now?"

Standing up, she turned towards Cardio, then stiffly turned back towards her desk. She put her hand on the zip-front sweatshirt draped over the back of her chair. Then took her hand off of the sweatshirt and turned back to Cardio.

"It is a tiny bit below comfortable temperature outside, particularly in the shade this morning," Cardio said. He was wearing a cardigan sweater himself.

"Won't kill me." She left the sweatshirt. The two turned towards the elevators. They did not speak for the trip down and as they strode through the small, quiet lobby.

Two people walking without purpose can be awkward. At any intersection they could each wait for the other to determine a direction. An anxious person will be always hoping that the decision is smoothly made.

Without speaking, Cherry and Cardio decided that it was best for Cardio to make any navigation decisions. In the midst of any gesticulation, he would point the direction he would like to go. That meant simply extending his arm before him and tilting his wrist left or right.

"Cherry, it has been two years since you started working with me here at The Green Paintbrush. What a journey it has been, eh?" Cardio turned them past the corner bar that The Green Paintbrush employees often headed to after work.

"Has? Past tense?"

"Not in the sense that it is over, but that it must change, Cherry."

"Please explain."

"I shall, I shall. Cherry, I am leaving Spokane and The Green Paintbrush. Although I will continue to own the business and take an interest in it, my involvement will greatly diminish."

Cherry looked ahead. Cardio's hand made a chopping motion to indicate that they would continue across the street at the intersection. They were leaving the commercial street of stone buildings that look down upon you. Houses were set back behind front lawns on both sides of the street, on their heels viewing the passerby across the expanse.

She thinks for a second. "You have put in place salespeople who can gather new business on the reputation you have built. Blaine ably manages existing projects. The designers that have been here over a year all provide pretty consistent work that suits Green Paintbrush style."

"The Green Paintbrush can probably continue forward successfully, it is true. It is now applying D equals R times T consistently to solve problems that matter. The project is, in a sense completed. By that I mean *my* project."

"Do you expect my role to change?"

"Cherry, you were my first significant hire. As you have seen, I needed people like you in order to make this project thrive. You were the proof to the theory."

"Where are you going?"

"Los Angeles."

"What will you be doing?"

"Cherry, I am not quite sure. While The Green Paintbrush has become just about what I pictured a few years ago, I am not what I was at that time. I need a new project. I am not quite sure what that will be, though I have some next steps in mind." His face lifted up slightly and away from Cherry. At the intersection he made no hand motion. The two sets of feet stuttered briefly then continued forward, across another street.

"Why are you telling me personally?"

"I do not quite know, Cherry. As you ask, I consider that it is because I want to impart some advice to you or share some feeling or sense. I am not sure what that would be exactly. But here we are, two friends taking a walk on a lovely day." He smiled as he turned to her. She took a second to smile back and broke his gaze rather too quickly.

Later that day, she received an email from Cardio.

Cherry, thank you for taking the time with me today. I realized that I am not quite sure what I am doing and that is quite surprising, quite unlike me.

I feel close to you because you responded to my teaching in a way that I had not expected. Teaching you, first in class and then here at The Green Paintbrush, was never a chore. I had planned to simply create people who would behave in the appropriate way, who would make correct decisions. I found that a strangely satisfying feeling would come over me when I saw evidence of higher learning in students and young employees.

When they would apply a recently learned concept or synthesize new ideas into something unexpected I felt, not proud, but that I had done something good – I felt that it was a worthy effort with worthwhile output.

I have so much gratitude to you, Cherry.

Cherry took the rest of that day off, which caused The Green Paintbrush to delay the presentation of the personal network concept for a client.

25

REGINALD *in* CHARLESTON

[MAYBE 2011]

REGINALD wakes. This keeps happening. This time an alarm awakens him, an unfamiliar alarm from his new phone. After he becomes conscious enough to know what is happening, he reaches up and above his head to the shelf at the top of his bed.

Prepositions often assume we are standing. Perhaps it is behind his head.

He locates the phone by texture and shape. It is plugged in at the bottom to a very short cord. He needs to view it to disable the sound. He cannot view it without unplugging the damn thing. Unplugging it properly requires two hands. What an intrusive design. Perfect for an alarm clock.

In the last few months, he has come to rely upon and even battle against the clock. Reginald uses the snooze function some mornings, waiting for something to occur to him that should compel him to rise.

Coffee would taste good right now. Perhaps there is something unexpected in my email inbox. Something like that.

Today he is not particularly troubled with rising. His dreams last night threaded the end of yesterday's work to today's. Today promises to be interesting.

He drinks the coffee he made and reads email off of the new phone. There is nothing surprising to read, but he enjoys the discovery of the new user interface, the hard surface of the touch screen, the casual motions of his hand that move the list of messages up and down.

He tries to swipe a message to one side, thinking that should have some symbolic effect; delete or file or something. Nothing happens.

For breakfast, Reginald splits a bagel in two and smears each side with a thick, even swirl of cream cheese. He puts one half into his microwave for 32 seconds. It is just warm enough that he can touch it. He removes it and puts the other half into the microwave but does not start the microwave, then starts to eat the heated first half.

Reginald was never a celiac, it turns out. His body was just very unhappy in Spokane. Since living in Charleston he has taken to pancake breakfasts, thick breaded sandwiches, and regular doses of pizza. His body has no complaints that he cares to note.

Microwave bagels have the perfect texture, but only for about 45 seconds. Then they harden horribly. He pushes the start button to heat the second half as he is finishing the last bite of the still warm first.

He is standing in the small kitchen space of a small, old apartment in Charleston, South Carolina. His bicycle is leaned against the wall in the dining nook, the same bicycle that crouched in a Spokane apartment six months ago.

A couple of years ago, Reginald had read on the Internet both personal reports and medical descriptions of celiac symptoms and diagnosed himself. He feels pretty funny about it, but no one here knows that he used to avoid wheat. It is not as common an occurrence in the South as it was in the Northwest. Talking about the misdiagnosis sounded unpleasant. He would have admitted fault and that makes him a bit uncomfortable. Doesn't it everyone?

He picks up his phone again to check the time. He will need to get to the office of SigmaShift Enterprises, his new employer.

SigmaShift hired Reginald based on his pedigree at The Green Paintbrush. The company has been in existence for forty years, evolving names as it has evolved lines of business. The founder had developed a dispenser that made it easier for assembly line workers to grab a single bolt. At the time the company was eponymously named Townshend and Associates.

While selling these dispensers to Detroit assembly lines in the 1960s, Riley Townshend noted other processes that he could improve. Soon the car companies would hire him to walk up and down their factory floors, taking notes on his preferred paper – a blue-lined quadrille pad on an aluminum flip-open clipboard. Then he would spend a half a day in a small office on-site where he sketched and documented methods to improve the process.

Riley resisted all attempts to hire him or to be trapped into exclusive contracts. He worked for everyone. Based on some records that Riley kept, Townshend and Associates later estimated that Riley's efficiencies over the 10-year period from 1964 to 1974 had resulted in a 0.1% increase in US GDP.

As computers became a part of automation in the 80s, the firm's consultants partnered with a research and development lab to create robots able to perform rudimentary tasks. A few years after Riley's death, the company renamed itself Process Shift, Inc. and went public. It populated its board of directors with investment bankers and car industry executives.

These executives felt that the service model meant that the company was constantly reliant on the good behavior of people – the company's expert consultants who offered custom service to each client – and company culture. Without both good people and a consistent culture that continued to honor Riley's model, the company would fail and have no value. In 1990, They hired a consultant to determine how to solidify the company and grow the value of the stock.

That consultant came into the boardroom and asked insightful questions about the desires of the board. He used terms that they were familiar with, often saying them in situations that surprised and pleased the board members. When they spoke, he made eye contact, nodded, and then took notes.

He left the meeting in Charleston, drove his rented car to the airport, and flew to New York. At La Guardia, he took a taxi to the front of a tall building. He rode the elevator to a middle altitude and walked into an office. There was a small, unattended reception desk. On top of the desk was a plastic pot of silk flowers and a very large silver call bell such as one would find on the front desk of a hotel for giants. The door to the inner office was opened and one could see inside a large, circular glass topped table with no chairs around it, but a variety of papers spread across it.

"Welcome, Don."

Cardio came out of a door to Don's left, clearly a small bathroom. In contrast to the formality of their handshake greeting, two faces of the old friends projected warmth and happiness to once again be together.

Cardio put his hand on Don's back and guided him through the office door ahead of him, stepped through, and closed the door behind them.

Reginald knew nothing of this story, but knew that in the mid-90s the company not yet named SigmaShift started developing software that it licenses to largely the automotive industry. This software has evolved. The initial offering provided inventory tracking of the component parts needed for each car. There were other companies that had made software to track inventory. One of these applications could spit out extensive tables of text and numbers that used a complex two-letter coding system to evaluate supply levels.

Process Shift, Inc. made use of the graphic user interfaces built into modern computer operating systems. Its reports were color-coded rows of cars on a calendar. If a car on the date was red, it meant that car could not be built with the current supplies. If the user clicked on that car, a window would pop up telling the user that on this date the factory would be out of, say, catalytic converter mount plates.

The board was very happy that the company pivoted so gracefully to selling software on recurring annual licenses. The stock rose. Don was thanked and referred to other boards populated by friends of Process Shift, Inc board members. His consultancy grew.

Reginald was aware of the history of the company, though neither Don's nor Cardio's name appears in the account he read. He did know the company main revenue was now software. In addition to inventory tracking, their software controls robots and analyzes productivity. In 2002, A defect poorly welded 3,000 engine mounts resulting in PR and legal headaches. The company changed its name to SigmaShift.

Reginald took his second bagel half into the front room of his apartment. There was no framed art on the walls, but one wall has a series of pieces of paper and glossy photographs stuck to it. Reginald has discovered that one can purchase a sticky, reusable gum-like substance that affixes light items to a wall, and then can be removed at any time. The papers are curled off of the wall a little bit. They are wrinkled and irregularly spaced.

The photographs are arranged roughly evenly spaced at eye height. The most leftward, farthest from the window and front door, is a low angle picture of an Arctic Circle drive-thru chicken, taken in the perfect glow of a desert dusk, set against a curious sky. Above and below are scraps of paper that read

“*First wheat*”

“*Traffic incident: speeder in blind spot*”

“*Interactions: 4-*

Grocery store checker

Gas station attendant

Motel reception

Fast food server”

“*Bad writing, success*”

Reginald pulled out his phone to check the time. He was now on the clock, billing for SigmaShift.

26

CARDIO TEACHING, LOS ANGELES

[2010]

IN the small classroom, Cardio felt very large, like he was occupying the bulk of it and all the students were smashed together in the leftover space.

He held a dry erase pen, blue. He has two others in his jacket pocket. They are of a different brand than the school provides, but they are his preference.

"Social change is often initiated by students, this recurs enough in history that it is almost expected that, when called upon, the student population will stream from their classrooms and onto the street, occupying buildings, chanting rhythmically, and waving clever signs.

"It is often assumed that this is a natural outgrowth of youthful inexperience, ideals not yet crushed by reality," he says. He has cradled the pen in front of him in the palm of both of his hands. It seems something like a holy relic, an offering to the class, his manner alone affixing significance to an everyday object. "Perhaps. But note that these movements are not necessarily liberal."

"The Iranian Revolution of 1979 inspired that nation to religious fundamentalism by a movement of college students who left class to occupy buildings. And certainly your understanding of history and people would be extremely simplistic if you believed that all Hitler Youth and young brownshirts were simply brainwashed through some magical spell.

They were activist youths as well." It was mid afternoon, a class time that famously inspired snoozing. Cardio took that as a challenge and worked his lectures into a manner which he hoped could keep the younger members of the class attentive enough to skip the nap.

"So, why are students so often the source of such change? It is a question normally solved with broad social and demographic information, but no effective proofs – at least not to my satisfaction.

"It would be difficult to create and test a scientific theory about this, but perhaps instead we could build a plausible model and utilize it for prediction until it no longer works. At that point, we can modify the model or discard it. No harm done to actual students!"

There is some chortling. Just the right amount of chortling. It does not slow his presentation but keeps the less intellectually engaged students attentive. Cardio turns to the dry erase board behind him. He draws a vertical line with the blue marker down the middle of the board. On the left he draws a very large square.

"The unit for sociological study is a category of people, a very big box. However, members of that category are also members of other categories. A person is a student, but also, say an animal lover and a celiac and a Portuguese."

He draws a number of intersecting and overlapping boxes, circles, triangles

"Which category or categories matter to the question at hand? It seems confusing and vague to me, not a model that we can use to predict much of anything. Perhaps instead we could create a model that does not shy away from the individual, the unit that actually makes decisions and is harder to divide up – at least without power tools and sociopathic tendencies."

He did not slow down for the few chuckles he got for the joke, but turned back to the dry erase board. On the right of his boundary he draws a simple outline of the bust of a person.

"We could interview individual student activists and ask them about themselves. What questions should we ask them?"

A woman in her mid twenties wearing two unmatched tank tops lifts her head from her notes. With an inheld breath she flips the end of her pen towards Cardio and then says, "Start with whether they fit the profile of activist, I think. 'Do you participate in protests or movements?'"

Another woman turned to the first speaker and said, “Sure, then we can start surveying them for suspected attributes, such as, I don’t know, ‘How much money do your parents earn?’”

Cardio knows that statistically across all university students women tend to speak less and for shorter times than men. He assiduously tracks gender participation in his own classes. It is pleasing to note that two women started out the conversation. He writes down their questions beside the drawing of a person. More questions come.

“Did you grow up near your university?”

“What is your GPA?”

“Do you like your father?”

“Wow, that would be pretty loaded.”

Others follow. Cardio writes down most of them. “Very good,” he says, “what about – and he writes as he talks, but not assuming that semi-staccato voice that people often use when writing in public as it is an unnecessary cue, “what color are your eyes?”

Everyone chortles and stops. “How can that...” is all the first woman says, then pushes the tip of her pen against her lower lip, scowling.

“Oh, all of these questions we have been throwing out are based on our assumptions, right?” The query comes from a boy in his very early twenties wearing a flannel shirt unbuttoned over a very white t-shirt. The boy usually wore similar outfits when he came to class. Cardio pictured him unwrapping a new white shirt from a plastic package every morning. “We, we, we run a risk of of of either proving we are right or else deciding the data is garbage, like in the bit from that Harvard thing you were talking about.”

“So we should test our testing by seeing if we can create nonsense correlations?”

Cardio puts the colored pen into his pocket. “I believe that I recently heard it put this way: ‘exactamundo.’ We have a pretty interesting study here. I must admit that I am curious, even passionate about revising this model of social divination (he points at the series of shapes) and have perhaps driven this class to think my model instead of creating your own. Perhaps, indeed, I have forced an assumption down your throat, sweetened secretly with a proverbial spoonful of sugar.

“Perhaps – in fact quite likely – I have not had some original and innovative thought here. For next class discussion, please seek out examples of studies or essays or other thinkings that build outward from the individual instead of inward from the population. I promise that I will not yammer so much."

Cardio had noticed that use of idioms and slang words that sound incongruent to his careful speech patterns create engagement with students. He tries not to practice this technique in excess. He enjoys the dislocated feeling himself.

After class, and after a short talk with the pen-wielding student about sociology journals – Cardio feels that if you are going to study that field, there are a couple of journals to avoid due to their less rigorous practice – Cardio turned on his cell phone and headed towards his car.

He was walking across the small grass courtyard in front of the classroom when the phone completed booting up and checked for any messages or missed calls. It beeped as he reached the concrete garage structure.

Cardio could have paused outside of the garage to listen to the message or he could go into the structure where he had no reception, collected his car, and then listened to the message as he pulled out onto the street, ably manipulating both the large automotive machine and the small communication machine.

Cardio did neither. He put the phone back into his bag and got into his car. He navigated the Los Angeles freeways just as traffic was thickening for the afternoon commute. Although traffic jams were notably reduced after the introduction of Clean and Sane Roads, the volume of cars continued to increase and traffic slowed every day anyway across America's urban centers. So many years later, urban Americans still tuned their radios to a station with frequent traffic reports, took a shallow breath, and entered the uncertain flow of traffic.

Cardio thought about traffic often. Although he felt that Don was the true father of Clean and Sane, he felt a... perhaps a godfather-like relationship to that hallmark law. He has now found himself a citizen of the greatest driving city in the world. It is easy to imagine that when he finds himself in traffic he sometimes thinks upon traffic.

With nothing else particularly troubling his mind, his thinking remained in the present. As he took a left turn out of the parking garage, he idly thought about a theoretical world in which that left turn would never happen. He imagined if for hours and hours the random flow of traffic, the decisions of thousands of individuals to leave their house, their work, their place of recreation, resulted in no reasonable path through the two oncoming lanes and no gap to enter the flow of his desired lane.

He felt this mental exercise cause him some consternation. He wondered if that was from the frustration he has experienced before when looking upon flawed systems or if it was the nature of a self who was denied what it wanted – in this case a simulated self that wanted to take a left turn. Cardio found it hard to divide those selves and isolate the unhappy feeling. He allowed the simulation and the feeling to blow away. An opening occurred and he turned into traffic.

He drove past the La Brea Tar Pits to his 1920s apartment building off Vincente Boulevard. Sitting on the stoop of the pink two-story building was Dr. Richie, a dreadlocked doctorate in critical theory and also a resident of the building. He was smoking a joint.

"Hello and good afternoon professor," Richie frequently addressed Cardio as professor, building an affinity between the two.

"And good afternoon to you, professor," Cardio knew that it gave Richie some satisfaction to have the affectation returned. Cardio strode past. There was plenty of space for Cardio to walk by, but Richie leaned slightly, signaling intent to be less in the way.

As the building door closed, Richie heard Cardio remark to himself, "a queer social nor-"

The door of Cardio's apartment opens onto a perpendicular hallway. One direction heads toward the kitchen and front room while the other towards the bathroom and bedroom. As a result, the first experience of the apartment is the opposite wall of the hallway. To combat the somewhat negative experience of opening a door to find a wall, Cardio has hung three items to be faced with when one opens the front door. After two framed mirrors (one tall in a wooden gilt frame and one square in a metallic frame), he has hung an empty frame made of a stark black metal.

It took some doing for one man who is not very adept at hands-on work to shim the two mirrors and point them so that the person entering the room regards their face in both.

Cardio makes coffee, sits at his small circular kitchenette table, and plays the voicemail message.

"Cardio, this is Carl, Carl Stoner. I hope you are well, yes. We first met, you and I, when we were both working on Clean and Sane Roads, back in the early eighties, through Don. Remember that? My, the times have changed, eh? Anyway, I tracked you down because I am working on a similar project, something a little bigger actually, but in the same vein. We could really use your skillset and I don't think it would take too much time away from your teaching, which I know is important to you.

"Please give me a call. I am in San Francisco today but will be driving to Los Angeles tonight. Let's get a dinner tomorrow."

Blaine was coming in to town tomorrow, but Cardio could skip dinner together. Blaine would probably appreciate the opportunity to explore Los Angeles a bit on his own. Cardio swirled the coffee in his cup, looked around his small apartment. He picked up his phone and dialed Carl.

27

MARY WAKES UP

[2010]

SHE woke up surprised. She usually does. That it happened at all, that it happened again. She enjoys, she had to admit, the panic. She had a vague idea that she was going to collect herself, form herself again. That this shock of being would fade.

It was a harmless apartment. She kept it dingy but not too cluttered. She did not like things in particular. If there was a reason to get rid of something, she would do it.

Things are heavy, and she is pretty weak. She can't walk too far, so she has the wheelchair. It is by the door. She doesn't use it in the apartment.

Her albums still sell, and it provides the better part of a living, but not quite enough to thrive or to make a change. She wonders sometimes if she will be lucky enough to fade before her art does. Living with little has some dignity, living with nothing...

She does not miss anyone in particular, she has not thought much about the difference. She did not see well back then. Her memory is of particular moments. She does not remember trends or statistics of her time. Touring. Studios. They happened. Interviews for all these different media. Those happened. How frequently, for how long – that is gone. She does not try to recover it.

Some people thought that a bad memory was a drawback, but she found it has its blessings. Like now. Today started out with the usual terror of awareness, but as an identity forms it looks forward, not backwards. Memory is where you keep your sadness. She looks into the emerging future.

She looks a fool sometimes, its true. She will come home with a dozen eggs two days in a row. She stacks them in the fridge and forgets about them, then comes home with a third carton two days later.

This day is not a special feeling day, but it has a something. A tolerable pressure on her skin. She watches it pass through her mind, the moment of the day that she has woke up into.

She has no where to go. This keeps happening. She will go anyway.

28

the EFFECTS *of* CLEAR *and* SANE

OTHER than a way to spice up a boring conversation, a real world what-if scenario is usually a giant waste of time. For instance, asking "what if America had not entered the Vietnam conflict?" stimulates untestable and unprovable hunches about culture, music, etc. However, for the sake of our conversation, what if Clear and Sane had never passed?

The effect on traffic is somewhat easy to deduce by multiplying the pre-1983 traffic congestion data by increases in population density. We could calculate the reduced collision incidents in a similar manner.

There are other variations in culture that might be harder to correlate. What of Don's claims of sanity? Did the country become less neurotic? Cardio tends to shy away from the newer, fuzzier quantifications such as attempts to quantify happiness. They contain too many assumptions for his comfort. Other quantified indicators can be a little more actionable, he feels.

One evening, while tweaking a geo spatial statistics user interface, Cardio was able to detect a change in the slope of suicide rates in densely populated areas starting in 1984. Perhaps...

With the swell of the Reagan boom, he could not identify any uptick in GDP. He left that alone. He tried instead to put his finger on some other information, wondering how the river that is the country bent around the Clear and Sane Bill.

Would the Honest Language movement have been motivated to change the FCC's policy on profanity?

Would the American car industry have pivoted so dramatically in the late 80s to develop small and efficient cars? How would the array of experimental fuel vehicles, such as electrical, hybrid, and fuel cell, been received in the early part of the century if our roads were still raceways?

Cardio worked up a calculation that projected fuel usage for the current population if cars had maintained their overpowered engines and performance tuning. He came up with an ungodly number. What would our relationship to oil-producing countries be like if things had continued?

This idle computation would sometimes fill Cardio's hours between class preparation and sleep. He saved the conclusions off in files on his local drive, which automatically mirrored itself to a storage service over the Internet. That storage service replicated his ideas on a number of servers spread throughout the world, then regularly backed up the entire collection to non-volatile media, which was safely archived.

29

CHERRY *in* SPOKANE

[2006]

THE changes around her were subtle after Cardio left, but Cherry noticed. Fewer meetings occurred around the tall table and more were held in the closed-off conference rooms. Sales people started bringing in uninteresting but high profit projects. The Green Paintbrush staff found itself relating to swaths of middle management from large corporations, wrapped up in conference calls of twenty people, bending over the conference phone and microphone, stuttering in tandem with a person in Turin, trying to figure which of you had something to say and which just wanted to hear themselves talk – to know that however painful and absurd the situation, however broken this felt, however far from reasonable this group-think practice was, you were alive within it.

Just about every day, some of the group would be found gathered at the bar around the corner just after work. Gifford, a graphic designer with an English degree, took to calling the place Conference Room D, but none of the veteran staff would take up his moniker. They preferred to just call it "there" with "there" loaded heavily with emphasis.

"Will I see you **there**?"

"I went **there** yesterday. I need to go home to the hubby tonight."

Cherry would be easily called to just about any meeting **there.** Her somewhat senior pay and single status meant that large bar tabs did not significantly cut into her income.

She walked home one cold January night, the short distance to her own upstairs downtown apartment. She was in short sleeves and a long cotton dress. It was well below freezing.

After the goose pimples, the flesh on her arms started to tremble. She had learned to not fight the trembling, it stimulates some amount of warmth. She had learned to not panic when her arms start shaking but to know that this feeling is transient, that her life is not at risk. Keep walking.

No one followed her.

In three years at The Green Paintbrush, Cherry had gained a little weight. Her legs were thick. A fold of fat formed above her waist when she bent to one side. It surprised her at first, but she computed that her activity level had slightly reduced after she left college. Going **there** so many nights a week was a clear source of calories she had not consumed before. The weight gain made sense.

It did not particularly trouble Cherry, but she could not avoid the fact that she would no doubt continue to fatten if her lifestyle continued. She made adjustments. Her drink of choice became gin and tonic. She sought exercise.

The best exercise for her was walking. Low impact, not athletic per se and god knows she had the time. In the mornings she would stroll out her front door for 45 minutes around downtown. Most weekends Cherry would head out to the mountain or countryside. With a light meal in a small backpack, she would walk alone to locations called out by guidebooks or strike out on an interesting road without much idea where she would end up.

30

CARDIO *and* REGINALD

[2011]

CARDIO could not get a song out of his head. It had been playing in a deli when he was in line. He was able to hear the entire song and, lacking anything else to focus upon, he listened quite carefully.

The song was structured with a refrain that repeated every other line of each verse, preceded by a drum cue that changed very little. The same phrase concluded the chorus. The singer was able to repeat the refrain in just about an identical manner until the last time through the verse where, due to a change in history, the word baby meant infant instead of loved one. The music became more poignant and the singer's voice cracked subtly.

The refrain, heard so many times, became embedded in Cardio's thoughts. Whenever he was not thinking about another thing, the refrain would return and fill the void. Later in that day, the percussion created by a student turning a knob and pulling open the door sounded enough like the drum cue that the refrain crushed Cardio's current thought, requiring his mind to complete the line.

Cardio was put on edge by the pop song.

He closed the door of his office. A meeting appointment pop up persisted on his computer screen.

Autonomy Conference Call, 9am PDT

Cardio picked up the desk phone and dialed. After one ring, an automated voice welcomed him to the conference call service. He looked up at his computer screen one more time to learn the pin number required to enter the conference call. He entered the number and then, while listening to the conference call preamble pre-recorded voice he scanned down the other invitees in the meeting appointment. Reginald's name was nestled in the midst.

Ding. "Who just joined?"

He wondered if Reginald had noticed Cardio's name on the appointment or if this would be a surprise. He supposed that Reginald had read through the participant's list prior to the call.

"This is Cardio Plathemy." He wondered if any of the ricocheting "Hi Cardio" was Reginald. He supposed that Reginald would not bother to join in the chorus.

Carl came on, breathing in audibly. "Cardio is a consultant that will be working some, ah, I guess actuarial and analysis for us. He will be sitting in on some of these calls." It struck Cardio how much older Carl sounded, and he wondered whether his own voice had aged. He was relatively certain that Carl was the oldest person on the call and Cardio the second. By, as they say, a country mile.

"Hello everyone." Cardio had opened up a browser and was looking up Reginald to discover if he was working still at the same organization. Yes. SigmaShift still claims him.

Carl seemed to be in charge of this call. "The other person I want to introduce is here in the room with me. Laney is a project manager who will be taking over that responsibility."

Laney's voice was chipper and fresh. "Can everyone see my screen? The clients have looked over the draft recommendations from Julie that we polished off late last week. She is looking at their revisions and working to develop a draft for internal."

"Excuse me, Laney, this is the new fellow Cardio. So sorry to interrupt, but you said 'see my screen.' I am afraid that I can't. I believe that you are using some sort of application which allows us to all see your computer display over the Internet, but I am not familiar with it. What is the process for this?"

There was a pause. "No problem, Cardio. Are you in front of a computer?"

"Yes, I am"

"OK. Click the link in the email."

"I am sorry, which email?"

"It was the thread from Tuesday, the subject line is something like 'version for review.'"

A small window appeared on Cardio's computer screen:

Chat Invitation From Reginald C. **Accept?**

Cardio clicked Accept.

Reginald C.: **Click here:**

And a long string of characters appeared.

Reginald C.: **And find your personal code in the meeting invitation, an email subject line "ConfiMeet Scheduled" dated 11:42 EDT Tuesday.**

Cardio did as he was told, locating his personal code in the email and successfully logging in to the screen share. It took half a minute, during which the meeting was largely silent.

"OK, I have it. Please continue."

"Great. No problem," said Laney. Her screen was a fuzzy spreadsheet with very small text. There was a color coding of some sort in action, different browns and reds imposed on some cells in one column. Cardio could not make out the grid's purpose. Laney did not declare it. "As I was saying, Julie's draft has been reviewed and is back in her hands."

Cardio: **Thank You. May I ask you a question?**

Reginald C.: **Yes go ahead.**

Cardio: **What is this spreadsheet?**

Reginald C.: **A talisman of the secret tribe of Projecta Manageria.**

Reginald C.: **Tribespeople believe that it holds magical powers to make those whose names are writ upon it do the bearer's bidding.**

Cardio emitted a big joyful laugh. Laney stopped herself. "I'm sorry?"

"Oh, please excuse me," said Cardio. The meeting was briefly occupied by a chorus of chortles. Cardio wondered if his desk phone had a mute button. He had not needed to mute before and worried that a miss-key would disconnect him from the call. Instead he closed the chat window.

With a forced staccato laugh, Laney continued. Cardio stopped watching her screen and attended to his notes. He wrote

> **Learn to mute**

> **Letter to Reginald**

He tapped out the song refrain with the butt of his pen softly, hoping that Laney could not hear.

Putta put, putta put put, putta put, putta put put.

31

REGINALD *at* SIGMASHIFT

[2011]

AT the conclusion of the conference call, Reginald disconnected the headset from first his phone and then from his ear. He was alone in a conference room at the SigmaShift office. Across the room was a bookshelf containing the colorful spines of technical manuals. They were largely documentation for extremely out of date software languages.

Reginald tapped his pen rhythmically as he watched the participants disappear from the listing on his screen. He pictured each one diving off the side of a ship into the ocean, a warm moonlit night, all in formal attire.

Eventually the roster disappears from the screen and another window appears saying "The Moderator has closed the conference." Reginald notes the unnecessary capitalization with a modicum of disgust.

Putta put, putta put put, putta put, putta put put. He taps out with his pen. With his other hand he uses a shortcut key to bring up his calendar. It is a little after 1pm, Eastern Standard. A thin red horizontal bar represents the current time. The bar lowers itself through the highlighted day. It is currently over a blank area but at 1:30 pm a maroon box labeled "UX D1 Review" awaits Reginald.

He sits and taps for a second. The only window in the room looks out to the bustle of the larger SigmaShift office space. With his free hand he swipes across the track pad of his computer to view his email application. There is a red 4 next to the envelope. Four new messages. He looks at the list. Two of them he archived after reading the first line. One he responded with a single sentence. One he read then marked unread so that he would be forced to return to it.

Reginald would like to stop thinking about the Autonomous project for a time. In the mornings, he stares at the half formed collage on his wall. His wall, that he comes to every morning, that he builds and turns and plans about and stands before, silently sipping water from a hazy pint glass.

He could open a blank book and write something for himself. Here is a city that he discovers every day, that he bikes across cobblestones older than the idea of united states, the view of the harbor Blackbeard held in siege, the bars where his new co-workers order shots "four ways" at the end of the night and then disappear, all solitary and chaste. He could write about the sonorous drawl of two Southern strangers exchanging pleasantries on the street.

And then himself. This Western US brain that is wandering this place, breathing this place, and why is he here at all? Did I just leave somewhere? Where was that which he left? Is this place even old enough for him?

He could pick up a pen and write something. There would be no witnesses. And yet and yet. He does not. He picks up the markers from the side table and the Post-it notes and works and reworks the timeline. The gaps shrink, then grow as he newly loves the use of glorious empty space, space for the mind to make its own, private decisions, to own the act.

He sits on his couch, trying to read Rilke, a long poem stretched over Greek legends, but his mind creeps away to the cockpit of a plane, to the role of the engineer of a train, and he opens a computer and searches for images and prints them and pastes them to the wall.

Here at the office no one knew about his wall of work in his living room. He had not had any visitors in his new apartment. It was presumed that he lived in a small place that was not great for hosting. Reginald was often surprised at how hospitality was administered here and frankly intimidated by it. He felt unprepared to offer the welcome, with drinks and snacks and space for sitting, that he received when he did get invites to his coworkers' homes.

He did not write, no. He did not change his thinking. He drifted off to sleep playing a question like a melody and woke to a possible answer and was testing the theory before breakfast. He found his email inbox compelling, so compelling. Outside experts contacted, internal timeline and scope conversations, drafts of designs discussed.

He checks his smartphone for new texts. Sometimes it fails to beep when one comes in. There are none.

Reginald pulls out a tattered notebook, almost completely empty of text. He thought about writing something but could not think of anything to write. *Putta put, putta put put, putta put, putta put put* he taps out on the surface of the book. *Putta put, putta put put, putta put, putta put put.*

He looks at the thin red line creeping down towards the next item on his calendar. The office outside continues to bustle. He scowls at his computer screen, which keeps people from waving at him through the window as they pass by.

He has time to polish his notes from the call before he moves on.

> AA: **Email Cardio**

Oh yes. He resolved to send a message of greeting to Cardio. There seems to be some significance to Cardio's appearance. Somehow. Reginald thinks that he needs to take some space to write something thoughtful. Does he have time now to make something significant?

New Message

No recipient.

"How interesting to hear your voice on the call this day, Cardio. I realized that I never responded to your very nice letter upon my departure from The Green Paintbrush. I suppose that I was quite moved by your message and felt that I could not equal it in impact. So, much delayed, thank you for your thoughts. Perhaps indeed we can meet in New York or some such place sometime soon.

As for the Autonomy project, I am glad to know your mind is involved. Perhaps you are not aware of my role: SigmaShift is offering user experience and automation thoughts about the individual user. We are not limiting ourselves to that scope, however. I have come to discover that the dramatic shifts in thought that we must accomplish mean that our work product must resonate – a word oft misused but please take it as an earnest choice in this situation. Resonate. Yes. The individual user must feel, as they experience autonomy, a thorough agreement with the experience. I write it down as a series of Yes: "Yes, and yes, and yes. Yes."

I am not an expert on the government relations (that means lobbying, right?) process but hopefully the yes and yes and yes can also be a part of what you are able to communicate and reach understanding about. This is what I mean about not limiting our scope. SigmaShift wants that yes and yes and yes to happen throughout the elements of Autonomy: Automation, user experience, messaging to the public, this government relations of yours and Carl's as well.

I look forward to working with you. Please feel free to reach out anytime. My contact information is below in my signature."

Reginald re-read the message and it was, though not perfect, destined to be effective. He put Cardio's email address in the "To" field and clicked send.

His computer and phone beeped, different tones, at nearly the same time. He had ten minutes until his next meeting and he had not yet compiled his notes.

32

CHERRY *in* SPOKANE STILL

[2011]

AS she walked up the last hill to her house, Cherry sang the last refrain and tapped out the rhythm on her thigh, *putta put, putta put put, putta put, putta put put*. She thought, "I want you not to be angry with me" as she breathed in and sang out, an octave higher than the original male voice, "And yes, I miss my baby."

The house was built in the 1920s, a bungalow with small rooms and many windows. Her porch, symmetrical and centered across the entrance, had half walls with siding identical to the rest of the house. She sees these half walls as arms coming from the house and offering an embrace whenever she arrives at the stairs.

Although the day was fading, she could feel the prickle of the 80-degree day still on her skin, particularly in light of the exertion of climbing the hill. It had been a long day and she welcomed the cool embrace of the house.

Cherry lived alone here. The built-ins in the living room displayed un-similar items she had accrued over her years in Spokane. She had no pets. She had recently broke off a relationship with a man ten years older than her.

Jim was the marketing director of the Spokane Winemakers. Just a few miles away from the more well known wine producing areas of Washington State, Jim's clients had a little bit of an uphill battle. He gamely organized local profile-raising evenings and took Spokane wines to food conventions throughout the world. Jim had certainly not made Spokane wines famous, but he was well liked by his clients and by the locals who attended his many food and wine events.

Cherry had met Jim at just such an event. She was very flattered by his attention. He quite formally and directly asked her for her number, if he could give her a call sometime. Less than a week later they went for a dinner together at a local fancy restaurant. Until they finished the first bottle of wine, the conversation was a sputtering candle. Eventually they found a rhythm of conversation. They were generally able to keep up that rhythm for the next nine months, particularly when there was wine involved. Lucky for their relationship, he had a ready supply of wine.

Cherry broke up with Jim because of how he spoke. For a month, she heard mounting evidence of an inner cruelty. She rarely felt anything but kindness directly from Jim and he certainly offered a caring self to the world in many situations. However, it became untenable for Cherry to hear conversations in which people not present were the needful victim of his stories, Jim's tools for affinity with whoever he was relating to.

"So this lazy-ass gas station attendant..."

Rang in her ears. She was with him when the attendant did not know the price of the energy beverage Jim wanted to buy. She watched him get steamed and berate the young boy. She felt her skin prickle when he raised his voice.

It was just two days later, on a coffee break from work that she told him she was not interested in continuing to see him. The experience occurred while the two of them were walking in the heat, he drinking a hot coffee and she drinking an iced latte from identical paper cups. She started the conversation four blocks from her office building. In the first block she did most of the talking. In the second block he asked some questions and she responded. The third block was mostly quiet between them, getting to the bottom of their drinks. It started to occur to Jim to respond cruelly on the corner where she turned, told him goodbye, and accelerated to the revolving door set into the old stone.

It has been so easy for Cherry this past year, so easy to see and decide. Her world has stopped being cloudy and confused. There are best options and we take them. It is like that.

There was a time, not too long ago, that Cherry would be angry after work, drinking. There because some limitation kept a project from being the best, the coolest thing it could be. Today, a user design project was scoped back massively because of changes in the client budget.

Between time and budget constraints, there is the best option. Between angry men and quiet nights at home, there is a best option. She could consider a what-if scenario, but there is no benefit to it. Today, she walked home in the heat, not thinking too much about work or about Jim. She thought of the heat, and of dinner, and of the smile of the new designer Hort, young and bubbly. Hort will be a fun girl to work with.

Collecting her dirty laundry from the pile in her bedroom closet, she found a shirt belonging to Jim. She immediately slips it into a manila envelope and addresses it to his house. It is easy to decide to temporarily stop the laundry process to take care of this other task. Coming up from her basement laundry, Cherry noticed the evening starting to come on, a late summer darkening. Not cooler, but the air starts to move through the neighborhood. She opens the big side window to try to feel it.

33

REGINALD WRITING

[2011]

REGINALD, since he was a teenager, could estimate the vintage of cars. It is not that he was in any way a car enthusiast. If he looked at a car, he could reliably figure the year that it was made. He did not have any certainty about what gave him this ability. A hatchback-looking Ford Mustang comes by and he thinks "1985." He does not check his ability very frequently against actual facts.

Should a car enthusiast note Reginald's ability, he would assume that Reginald tirelessly reads and catalogs car body styles. This is not the case. It is two factors that combine to give Reginald this prescience. First, he is very intuitive. That is, he will listen to and allow for thoughts that are not fully formed nor attached to a tangible fact. He allows his mind to make decisions that it cannot quite justify.

Secondly, he scrapes data from the world constantly. Reginald collects information as it occurs. He is not a compulsive reader but he does find it necessary to collect whatever information presents itself. As such, a film set in 1985 which has a person purchasing a new Mustang becomes a data source to Reginald. He may not remember the movie but he will remember the car shape and the number "1985."

Here in Charleston, he has considered continuing to write. After what happened as he was traveling across the country, there was not much reason to continue to write. The world did not wait for anything from him and those things that felt necessary to say were in fact nightmarish to consider verbalizing.

However, now he stared at the timeline before him every morning. It put everything into the right size and it was achievable. He could consider it and it would not bleed together into one horror. There was space before and space after.

Work had a consistency about it these days. A new corner came up every week. With Cardio a part of the effort now, SigmaShift project management was contorted trying to define the scope of Reginald's work as broadly as possible. They feared that Cardio's presence would erase their role as well as the significant stream of revenue and prestige associated with this job.

So he considered writing again. He had picked up some books to find inspiration. He found a book of essays by Octavio Paz and a slim book of poems by Richard Wilbur. He pawed them as he lay in bed. When he woke, before he got out of bed, he would sometimes reach for Wilbur and read a poem out loud, half awake.

He waited for a line of his own to come, for the writing to start. For there to be a marquee lit up in his mind with a phrase that needed to be written. All the phrases that needed to be written now were censored before they made it to the marquee. He could not state such things for the record.

One morning the timeline needs nothing and produces nothing. Reginald takes down a blank book, the kind he has preferred for writing poetry. He opens it to the first page. Like a minute spear, he wields a pen at his ear standing over the book. His hand pins it to his kitchen table.

The pen clicks open, closed, open.

He starts writing. With a great exhale he drops the pen to the paper and starts to put words together.

It is utterly uninspiring. He tools a few phrases. They work fine. He closes the book. It remains on his kitchen table as he finishes preparing for work. He pushes his bike out the front door by the seat, leaning it slightly to his hip when the steering starts to go askance. The book sits on the kitchen table, still closed.

It stays closed until dinner. After pouring his second glass of wine, Reginald opens the book to the first page and starts reading. The pen goes back to the ear and clicks intermittently. Occasionally it dives towards the paper. Reginald's head starts to crane forward. He pulls his chair tighter to the table. Pours a third glass. Tears out the page and refers to it as he writes another draft in the book. Closes the book and turns to his computer.

In a short second he is back to the book. Turns the page and tries out a phrase. Traces and retraces a three-line-high question mark in the right margin.

In the morning, instead of staring at the timeline, he input the new poem into his computer and sent it to a printer that clicked and hummed in a quiet corner of his living room. He pasted it to the wall facing the timeline using the same adhesive putty he had used to collect the timeline.

"It is not the same as it was," he later explained in his autobiography. He leaves out the essential secrets. "Writing was work, not in the least bit inspired or illuminated. Interesting work, but work nonetheless. When writing stopped being channeling – magic – it became useful silently." After there were five poems on that wall, he started sending them away for review. They were quickly accepted into journals.

Little changes for a newly published poet in America in the early decades of the 21st Century. He did not share the success of his publication with many people as it tends to confuse communication. "Oh, you are a poet," leads to an asinine conversation nine times out of ten. One out of ten people simply drop the topic gracefully. In the eyes surrounding him, Reginald preferred being a designer and user experience consultant to being a poet.

34

CARDIO GRASPING AUTONOMY

[2011]

CARDIO is having a coffee in an airy, crowded coffee shop off of Wilshire Boulevard. He holds a tablet PC and has before him a tablet of paper of the same dimension as the tablet. A pen is uncapped and lies diagonally across the paper. He has written an outline of sorts, however it is broken up with connective arrows. The pad looks like a football offensive play overlaid on a meeting agenda.

He taps the paper with the corner of the tablet PC. The data is convincing. Given an even playing field, what benevolent dictator would not choose autonomy? Lives saved, time saved, fuel saved. National ROI in eight years. Washing of hands motion. Done.

There are no benevolent dictators, and historic evidence suggests that actual collective decisions are never the best for the populace. They need a power play. As he thinks about it, they need an emotional play. He puts the tablet down and picks up the pen. With his free hand he flips to a blank piece of paper.

What good is the logic at all? He cannot dispose of it. The logic has got us this far, fueling the true believers. Ongoing, these facts need to be worded for them. He flips back to the first page and, for the true believers, puts a large + boldly at the top of the page. Once again to the blank page, he draws a horizontal rectangle and fills it in, a minus.

“Pluses for the minuses

+ Good deeds. For your elderly grand mother. For the next generation.

Low value. Self interest trumps in most situations.

Possibly additional justification with built momentum.

+ Evolutionary

Low value. Countered by “I value tradition.”

Believers will fill this in themselves.

Avoid.

+ New ability

Personalized

Learnable

Adaptable.

Competence opportunity.

Cardio sips his cooling coffee. He has been in the coffee shop for a while. He looks at the three headings. He holds the pen at his ear like a spear. Three times it stabs towards the paper but does not touch.

He lowers the pen to the table and sneaks it towards the bottom of the page. He circles New Ability then writes diagonally upward across the list “**Green Paintbrush**” in block characters.

35

BRADY *at* WORK

[2011]

HE still feels awkward in a suit, and it shows. Senator Brady Carson knows that this actually helps his efforts at times. He plays that in his favor rather than trying to overcome it.

His interns and staff are often better dressed than he. He sticks to off the shelf suits only modified if the cuff does not break right. His lead staffer bears himself in suits of subtle tint and careful cut. Brady can see the cost in them and indeed feels that they look great on James. However, he knows that for Brady to get what he is looking for, wearing bad suits awkwardly works just fine.

Any opponent, supporter, or undecided. Any person walking in to meet Senator Carson to convince or inform him. Any reporter. They all felt on equal or greater footing with him when they beheld his awkward suit.

He helped this on. Unless the heat of a Washington DC summer was unbearable, Senator Carson kept his ill-fitting jacket on. While all the men around him switched to shirtsleeves, sometimes just to clarify that they are able to be informal, he would stick to the jacket. Before resorting to removing the jacket in the face of heat or activity, he will first unbutton and allow the jacket to flap about him. He keeps heavy objects, notepads, pens, his wallet in the side pockets where they make his jacket sides swing like independent pendulums, unaware of each other.

You walk into a room and the very center of power is distracted, sticking his head out and down. Smiling and not making direct eye contact with you. His suit is bunching under his armpits. He reaches out a hand to shake yours and his unbuttoned coat folds out revealing the shiny liner. You are disarmed. You revise your introductory paragraph, the one you were planning, to use smaller words and get more quickly to the point. Dumb it down. Say your piece and get out of here.

But he is ready for you. Brady Carson reads his staff briefs, then follows up with his own research. He reads those things that support what he believes initially, then closes down his computer and lights a cigarette. He writes out what the opposition would believe. He opens the computer back up and researches again as the other point of view. If there are other parties affected, he will research as them. When preparing for a meeting, his goal is to think of a question that sounds harmless but gets a pause, a stammer, an original and unprepared thought.

To do this he needs to go beyond simply and just. He explores the peripherals of an issue. This is national politics. The peripherals are still lives and people's futures. He has come to understand that the central is just the most lucrative issue. The old saying: money talks.

Right now, James has stepped out of his office. He is alone for a second. There is a bit of time before the next meeting. He reads a news feed. Autonomy, it says. Autonomy.

36

REGINALD DREAMS *of* DRIVING

[2011]

HE is aware of the piece, even so far from it. Here at SigmaShift offices, he is aware that there is a part of a poem waiting for him.

But really, this time is for autonomy. That is a poem in itself. In recent meetings organizations' roles have become more defined, and cascading down SigmaShift has defined Reginald's role. It goes like this:

Right now Cardio is establishing the groundwork for communicating with first the sources of power and then the voices of power about autonomy. Meanwhile we need systems within the vehicles that are cohesive to a user, to all viable users. Identify these people and make them whole with an autonomous vehicle.

SigmaShift and their client have done a great deal of research into these people. At Reginald's fingertips are reams of fascinating studies and interviews with consumers. No cost was spared at the outset to collect consumer information. Instead of adopting one discipline about how to discern a consumer's tastes, SigmaShift and their client adopted at "360 degree" solution. Reginald thought that 360 degree was code for big, wasteful budget.

For most of the projects that Reginald has worked on, budgets and timelines did not allow for this quantity of research. Very frequently, someone from the client simply says "our clients are afraid of alligators" or something similar and that is the premise for his work. Even if there is early research, he has never been accountable to it.

He read some of the documents, even printed them out and took them to a bar. Technically against his contract and best practices, he felt that reading them among actual people who drove cars would better connect the research with his thinking.

He read that over 40% of drivers over fifty have anxiety about losing their driver's license as they age. He read that men secretly believe that women are the cause of traffic jams and that a notable minority of women agree.

He sipped a glass of wine and looked over the room. Sunlight passed through. Music played. People talked to each other and ordered drinks. No one was currently driving but they would all be getting behind the wheel soon enough.

He would not. He drove rarely. His expensive and small apartment was bike distance from work, just as he was in Spokane. Other than the moving truck he drove across country, he had driven once since he arrived.

Paige had curly hair, seemingly very thick but actually quite light in the hand. When they met he at first thought it was red but later realized that was a trick of the low lights and his high hopes. They talked until two and she took his hand as the lights came up (really auburn, not red at all, he thought). "I have a boat in the harbor. Come on." She turned and would have fallen back on to the old couch they had imprinted themselves upon but with her hand still in his, Reginald was able to tell her body which way was upright and keep her moving.

However, the idea of her driving did not sit well with Reginald. He gracefully took the keys and asked directions. While he was far from a legal driver, he felt that he had a much higher percentage probability of getting the two of them somewhere other than jail.

Her car was a stick. A pretty modern little thing with a digital screen in the middle of the dashboard. After he stuck the key in the ignition he watched the screen's complete boot up routine. He resisted the urge to take notes.

"Why do you have this car?"

"It gets me around." She smiled and pushed her thick hair behind one ear. A strand sprung out and bounced down between her eyes. She blinked a long blink, "I am paying on the loan. First time in my life I took out a loan on a car, but now that I have the bank job I felt it was, you know, time to have a grown up car."

"Bank job. You rob banks?" He winked and looked around for the headlight switch.

"Silly boy. You have said funnier things tonight. The lights are already on. Bella knows it is dark out."

He deduced that she named the car Bella, which he noted is a name common in Paige's grandmother's generation. He doubts many people his age named their cars Jennifer. "What else does Bella know? Does she know how to find us a jazz station?"

"Bella! Play XM. Jazz station." The screen in the dash displayed a simulation of an analog radio dial and the car was filled with saxophone.

"Nice job Bella." He put the car in reverse and backed slowly out of the spot. After shifting forward and then pulling onto the street, he said, "surprised you got a stick shift."

"I like the control." Another time she swept her hair behind her ear and gave a long slow blink. She put her hand on his thigh and tilted her chin forward. "hmmm."

He knew the place her boat was moored but, not owning a car, had never driven there. While she was watching his chin he drove past the parking entrance.

"Oh. No. It is back there." She pointed over her shoulder. He took a left turn into a gas station, pulled around, and got back on the road going the other way. It saddened him that instead of a single right turn he had to take two lefts.

His bag was in the back seat. In it was the research and his notes. He had not brought his computer, but he needed to remember that the very paper he carried was more valuable than an electronic device, that losing it or even letting someone see it was far more costly. Reginald has never really gotten used to seeing people spend money on what he does. He definitely is confused by the idea that it requires secrecy.

Though, he points out to himself, he has a couple secrets of his own. His private, multiple personality disorder board of directors is constantly strategizing how to maintain them.

She pointed him to her parking spot. When he turned the car off the screen went through a boot-down procedure, displaying a short graphic of the car they were in with the text "goodbye, thank you." It made him think ahead to tomorrow morning and he smiled. Paige was cute and smart. He was drunker than he had thought he was. It was a warm night. The water was across the parking lot. Down a ramp was boat after boat after boat in rows. Each was unique, chosen by a person and then customized to make them further a wish fulfillment.

It is nice for a piece of technology to say thank you. Technology should be nice.

37

CHERRY, *a* NEXT MORNING

[2022]

CHERRY woke, as always happens. On most mornings she does not need an alarm but drifts to consciousness when morning starts looming over the darkness. She thinks that is a nice phrase.

Morning looming over the darkness.

She drinks a glass of water set at her bedside table. With both feet on the ground, sitting on her bed, she takes five full, slow breaths. No one ever told her to do this.

Downstairs, she makes a small pot of loose leaf green tea in a sturdy ceramic pot. After the monitored steeping time (timed for buttery, not bitter) she transferred the tea to an insulated stainless steel thermos. It has a short but effective divot in the lip to allow for pouring without dripping down the sides. Cherry appreciates the feature. She makes and eats a small breakfast after pouring onc cup of stcaming tea into a hefty ceramic coffee cup. Its twin sits waiting in the office of The Green Paintbrush. She does not drink the scalding liquid until after the steam abates. Her eyelids half close, she takes in the buttery slide across her tongue. She playfully swishes the tea back and forth with her tongue. It crashes against one set of molars and then the opposite set. She has a little gum recession and there is a slight pain response on one side. She remembers that she has a dentist appointment later in the week.

She recalls that it is Tuesday. She has no meetings until the 11:15 round up, scheduled so that late risers and early birds can both make it at their best. Someone has a standing 11:30 meeting so the round up does not go over long most days.

Morning looming over the darkness.

Pretty. Is "looming" too much? Morning haunting...

Darkness, haunted by the morning.

She takes her cup of tea to a writing desk, where she collects some stationery and a pen.

Hey you glorious bastard

She writes, smiling.

I have one for you. Free to a friend in need of such things:

Morning looming over the darkness

I had considered

Darkness, hunted by the morning

But methinks that looming's slightly histrionic manner is not as detrimental as the tired hunting metaphor. You can have your pick, since you are the expert in this, the most boring of arts.

Hope you are well. Keep your dick in your pants! Keep an eye out for those hordes. See you in Chicago, perhaps.

Mine,

Cherry

38

THEY MEET *for the* FIRST TIME

[2011]

"I don't normally smoke, but New York seems to suit cigarettes." Cardio has pulled an elegant box from an inside pocket of his jacket as well as a bright yellow disposable lighter. Reginald is most taken aback by the unclassy nature of the lighter. Plastic, typical, short. It does not fit well in the hand and the color makes it look like a cartoon character drawn on top of a documentary about the Vietnam War.

"I didn't think you could smoke in bars here," said Reginald.

"This bar defies the law. They want to preserve The Old Ways." Cardio capitalized "The Old Ways" with intonation and eyebrows, "thank you for meeting me here."

"My pleasure, Cardio. I very much appreciate the invite. Never been to New York. I don't spend much time in big cities like this."

"What you fear in them is nothing. They function with the same proportion of chaos-to-order as Spokane and Charleston, Reginald." He exhaled gently, his face sinking into satisfaction. "And yet with a greater total quantity of humanity, big cities come to conclusions faster. They are a more efficient culture deciding machine than your middle-sized burbs."

"I had not thought of that. As you can imagine, your choice of the word efficiency appeals to me."

Cardio smiled and tapped the ash off his cigarette. Tipping it down at a 45 degree angle from the plate he had adopted as his ashtray, he spun the cherry to roll still more ash off and leave a pleasantly tapered cone of cinder. "Of course. You would also appreciate how a city offers more evidence to the observer, that one can draw conclusions with more data."

"I see."

The walls, the floor, the whole bar is splattered red. In the low light, the black painted elements tend to disappear except, due to the high gloss paint, swishes of white revealing wood grain or plaster texture. Reginald arrived on a plane earlier in the day. He flew over the tallest buildings in America, the twin towers at the southern tip of Manhattan, then swooped east to La Guardia. Then, a long taxi ride into Manhattan. His company had booked him in a small boutique hotel in Hell's Kitchen. Across the street was a large church, old and crouching, attended to by collections of homeless men.

Reginald made himself comfortable in his room. He texted Cardio to let him know that he arrived. Cardio responded "See you at the appointed time and place." Reginald got the idea that Cardio disliked the modern habit of constantly reconfirming and refining plans. He did not text further and instead plotted a dinner plan for himself. Something interesting but easy to find.

When they met, Cardio asked, "Where did you eat your dinner?"

"At Katz's. I guess it is famous."

"Yes it is. Great place."

"How can a place so accessible maintain fame? I mean, how can a place like Katz's exist for so long without being overrun, turned to a museum or a shadow of itself?"

"An interesting question. The market would not tolerate that, I suppose. Who would want fame if fame destroyed what it looked at? You, from the periscope of the submarine you exist in, see media reflections of the culture engines and you think you are looking clearly at the very thing." Cardio laughed, bouncing and closing his eyes. "These are people. They are living here, doing the what that fulfills them."

"Hmm." Reginald sipped his whiskey. He had had a previous whiskey at a less ostentatious bar down the street between his giant sandwich and arriving here. "Who are we meeting tomorrow?"

“We are meeting some lawyers who are working for some venture capitalists who may provide some capital for Autonomy. My concern is not the money but that they can help provide a different face for us. Not a large car company but innovative self starters. Incidentally they do their share for democracy by contributing heavily to political campaigns.”

Reginald looked around, then looked at Cardio. Cardio wore a light wool jacket over a button shirt. His hair was cropped a bit shorter than the picture on The Green Paintbrush website. As Reginald looked about, Cardio kept his eyes trained on Reginald, a clipped smile on his face. The cigarette smoldered, barely tended. Reginald felt like he was the most interesting thing in the room. “And what am I to do?”

“Reginald, you need to sound real smart but a little distracted, a little anti-social. You will be able to do this naturally. As some have said before, it is a part you were born to play.” With his wrist, Cardio lofted the cigarette first above his mouth, forehead level, and then lowered it into his lips.

Reginald breathed twice before responding. “Very well. Does the meeting have an agenda?”

“That would be pointless with these people, I am afraid. They will come in the door and start asking questions. No agenda would be adhered to or even read. These fellows don’t even know what their next appointment is until their phones beep and send them down the hall.”

“I see.” His whiskey was empty. Presuming that Cardio was paying the tab, he raised a finger and made eye contact with the bartender. Hell, he didn’t care who was paying or how much it cost. This place, far from home, was a wormhole, its own gravity and its own compass points. Coming across the town on the subway, finding the momentous sandwich, then striding this direction to a steep stairway was more fire in his belly than even when he moved to Charleston. The bartender just poured more whiskey into the glass and nodded while she did it. This was easy. He watched everything carefully.

Reginald woke again. It kept happening that way.

Before memories came to him, he had to figure out where he woke. The curtains were open, as was the window. Through the window, it was a gray day on a cramped outside patio. No view of a street but he could hear it past the opposite building. A plastered building. Multiple windows looking back at him, lying with half his face embedded in a very soft bed. New York City. Hell's Kitchen. 49th Street stop, just after Times Square.

He knew where he was, now he could get to remembering.

"Can you watch yourself?" said Cardio.

Reginald thought a great deal about himself. He considered his self observation to be much greater, more specific, and continual in comparison to what he perceived the general population practiced. At times he considered it somewhat egomaniacal. Yes, he watches himself all the time, he thought. Isn't that obvious, Cardio?

There were several whiskeys and a conversation that took concentration.

As he became again accustomed to breathing, as he noticed that one nostril was plugged with mucous, Reginald wondered what impression he left with Cardio. What did he say and speak about? Was he controlled?

And what time is the meeting? They had made arrangements to meet, but they were not coming to Reginald just now.

He had left his phone on and had forgot to plug it in to charge. That could become a logistical annoyance today.

1 new message from Cardio Plathemy.

"As agreed, I will see you at my favored brunch spot. I have emailed you the address and subway stop."

Thank you, Cardio. Bases covered.

He has time enough for a quick shower, but first he puts his phone on the charger. Even the 30 minutes of charge could simplify the rest of this day.

Should there be preparation for this meeting? Cardio seems to think that unnecessary, that in fact this meeting seemed functionally unnecessary. That this meeting had no function. Yes, without function. However, seemingly necessary. Is that a plausible differential? This is something being without function and yet necessary?

Nah. The function is a human experience, not a contribution to a quantifiable system. Reginald just does not instinctively put meaning (function) to such things. Cardio is willing. That is something to note.

After the shower he copies the address Cardio provides into a mapping application on his phone. All while tethered to the wall charger. Every second of charge a blessing for his future self, wandering this place in need of resources. Then he dresses, collects his luggage (the plan is to go straight to Penn Station from the meeting) and disgorges his self into a New York day.

39

THE TRAIN

[2011]

REGINALD reclines his seat and imagines what it is like to be loved.

The meeting was as Cardio predicted. Reginald did little but left feeling exhausted and confused. After a series of polite handshakes he found himself in a taxi to the train station, trying to recall some specific action to take following the meeting. Three men in shirts that perfectly suited them sat around a corner of the conference room. Cardio, Reginald, and a woman in a business suit sat scattered around the overly large table.

As the train starts banking momentum for the journey south, Reginald recalls parsing nonsensical sentences in his head throughout the meeting.

To be loved. It would feel like what? Like a certainty, perhaps. A knowing that one thing would not shift in the near term. Of course, love is limited by mortality, so it would only be certain for the period of time that both parties were alive.

Close your eyes. Take an emptying breath. Picture being loved. That would be having someone fully committed to your well-being. To know that someone is fully committed to your well-being: To be aware you are loved. To know that no matter your behavior or state, someone is willing to look out for you.

He wakes up briefly as the train stops around Washington DC. They are changing out the electric engines for diesel for the rest of the trip to Charleston. He misses Charleston a bit. In half a day, early in the morning, he will be back. A taxi from the train stop to his home. His bike will be in the hallway. The two walls of papers will be there. He can stand between them.

40

CARDIO TEACHING AGAIN

[2010]

"THERE'S this guy in downtown all the time, yelling about some sort of thing and he is so like him, but the obverse..."

"I am so pleased with the appropriate use of big words, Levi," Cardio immediately regretted his patriarchal tone, which has not shown to resonate with the modern college student. He has started saying to himself that his persona should be *distant scholar, formerly speaking askance, whose attention you have briefly attracted.* It makes them feel special but not the central subject, no pressure and not under an authority. However, he did need to redirect Levi. "I believe that I am one minute late. My apologies. I was speaking with a specialist. How they do carry on.

"Today might be one of those zero note days, I am happy to say. I must remember to build a couple of these into the syllabus in the future. Regardless, this point in your education and this point in my history as an educator both are served by this lecture. I do not expect you to have paper in front of you, unless drawing circles helps you to stay awake.

"For thousands of years, scientific inquiry and social movements were the province of the very rich. This means that the burden of martyring yourself on hard work and frustration was kept from the poor. While children of wealth and privilege were dawdling about asking 'why does light split into rainbows' and 'what happens if we ask the whole city's opinion before we invade our neighbor,' the children of the poor were able to engage in meaningful labor in an effort to keep themselves and their families alive and somewhat comfortable.

"Things have changed in the last couple hundred years. It is still highly unlikely that a truly poor – that is a typical – citizen of the world will rise to prominence in a way that notably alters history.

"I am sure you understand that when I say alters history I am touching on the sorts of topics that are in fact in the syllabus: social change, scientific discovery, insight that is reproducible and that creates meaning in multiple contexts.

"However, more than a few Cinderella stories exist of poor people who have gained an education and risen to prominence. We love Cinderella, so any physicist or politician or even writer whose background is even slightly hardscrabble will never escape that part of the narrative. Every introduction, every interview, and every obituary will mention their not-rich beginnings.

"As case studies, this is of course valuable. It proves that something is possible. However, such data is not consistently provided in these contexts. Being raised wealthy is not much of a story, so it is left out of the introduction, interview, and obituary of the vast majority of history shakers."

Cardio drew a set of parenthesis on the dry erase board, a recurring symbol in his lectures that he needs to insert information here that does not flow well. "Now then, another narrative – that of familial heritage – will be included in these quasi-examinations. We can glean from the fact that so and so was raised by a physicist and a professional tennis player that they had a lifestyle of privilege in some style." He drew a line through the parens.

"The stories of poor who get to work really hard and be frustrated and filled with doubt for most of their lives and then do something interesting for a moment and have an impact that changes the world long after they are dead is, while statistically insignificant, still important." Cardio paused and hefted the dry erase pen in his hand a couple of times. "It is significant to most everyone in this room, because it gives you a foolish hope. A hope that might be just powerful enough to allow for you to blindly overcome the probabilities and do something significant, create meaning for yourself in a larger sense than just feeding the family and perhaps having rather a fun time of it."

"Now, as I said, this narrative is relatively new. The folks I have lectured about from ancient China, South America, Persia, and the Mediterranean were pretty much all rich kids. And of course you know from your other classes that we don't mean middle class. We mean rich. Rolling in it. Ruling class. Buy and sell people kind of rich.

"This is not a class discussion that I want to have now. Please put down your Marx. What I want to talk about is the risk of specialization, in fact the damage that specialization is doing to your lives at this very moment. That, while the narrative that is most readily available is that of extreme specialization, multi-disciplinary work is what may yet save us from the holes that we are digging ourselves into.

"As poor and middle class students graduate with a narrative available to them of success and innovation and getting prizes from Nordic kings, they must work. As they are smart, they know before they graduate that work is their immediate future. As such, they make some sort of survey of the type of work available. That work story is the story of specialization, of focusing headlong into genetics, or gender studies, or nutrition, or whatever. They need to show that they can contribute to a tribe of people who speak a jargon and understand an arcane group of data. They train themselves to be specialists. They do this because they are smart and know that this is how they will succeed.

"And so they join the tribe. They learn the jargon. They buy into the import of their specialty. If they are good, the specialty rewards them with money and positive human attention. They cleave themselves to it in appreciation and they...succeed."

Cardio had practiced a bit for this part. He turned to the board and drew a hammer, the style that a carpenter would use with a claw on the back. For a quick gestural drawing it had a nice suggestion of dimension, though he did not spend any time on shading. He turns back to the class before he starts to speak again.

"There is a saying that when all you have is a hammer, every problem is a nail. This is a wise saying, and I hope you are seeing its relevance to our conversation this morning. There may be a time, maybe that time is today, when you realize that the world does not distill down to anything. Ever. That your specialty, your arena of knowledge, is not the bottom of the bowl. There is not a bottom to the bowl. There is not a bowl. That as you are scrapping for survival as a specialist, you are drawing hard, artificial lines around phenomena, calling them domains. You may in fact find yourself in turf wars with other specialties working on similar problems. You may compete for budget, for publication, for the attention of the industries that finance the actual implementation of any solution that you devise.

“You are hurting the world by specializing, by swinging this hammer. You are slowing discovery and innovation. Learn the disciplines of your neighbors and of your competitors.

“I bring this up because there has been great innovation in brain research coming out in the last few years. They have discovered that the brain can reform itself on the instruction of its owner. In an article this month in Schizophrenia Research (a highly specialized journal of that type of highly specialized journal which utilizes jargon and common presumption to move their conversation along) the author states...”

Cardio has crept over to the table in the corner. His leather book bag sits on its back so he can easily flip the top away. The journal is on the top, folded in half lengthwise like it is ready to swat a fly. Cardio does not open the journal but grips it like a hammer.

“ ‘Our understanding of the basis of schizophrenia has been completely undermined by the emerging research. We will need to reevaluate all of our assumptions going forward.’

“There are two things wrong with this. ONE. The writer uses the word ‘undermined’ which suggests that an outside actor had damaged the structure. In reality all that has happened is someone pointed out that the structure has always been unstable. TWO. That religion, philosophy, and folks working in learning research have known forever that the brain can be remapped. They did not know how to explain it in the jargon of a researcher of schizophrenia, so schizophrenia research went along with their theory that pathways in the brain are static.

“As a result, millions of people who suffer the horror of schizophrenia were told that their situation was intractable and the best thing to do was to take drugs which staunch their behavior somewhat.

“Specialization is a hammer, and when it is not driving nails it is breaking up people’s lives. Do keep this in mind. Even as I am teaching you, I am thinking that I need to rethink the hammers in my own life.”

Cardio looked down at himself, first at the journal that he had crushed in his hand, then at his chest and the foreshortened legs below that. He wondered if he was doing enough.

41

CARDIO *at* HOME *in* LA

[2011]

CARDIO has not yet started talking, he is just walking though downtown Los Angeles. A man is coming toward him. This man swings his arms back from his navel. Cardio strikes the small hand drum he is carrying with a stuffed monkey he swings by its legs. Now is as good a time. Now.

"Now is the good time, people, the time to love and to stop looking outside of now." He sticks his tongue out and lolls it across his face. It feels unusual, unique, and he laughs while he does it.

"Wherever you are going, it will be there when you get there, but here, here will be gone, my sisters and brothers. You are my sisters and my brothers, there is no way around that and so I am here to tell you about here. Here, and now.

"Are you thinking about what you are going to buy next? Why not think about what this strange man is saying to you? And why he is wearing these gorgeous threads?"

Cardio is wearing a red vest of a western style with a star made of sequins over the breast. He is wearing very large sunglasses that are asymmetrical, a model likely found in a vintage shop dedicated to the kitsch of the 1980s. He is also wearing a yellow speedo, which makes his thin and flexible legs seem shaky and unstable. He is not wearing anything else. His hair is contorted into a whorl.

"This drum," he bangs the drum again with the stuffed monkey, "this drum is now. It is also here. Do you know what else is both here and now? YOU! That is right, you and this drum are right here and right now. You know what else? I love you both. I love this drum. It calls out NOW NOW NOWNOW NOW NOW HEREHERE and I listen. I love you, you are beating as well, showing me new rhythms and cadence. And you are here right now. Here right now with me! This is just perfect!"

Some people stream by, most stay carefully out of the way of the swinging monkey. Some smile. Some frown. Many practice a looking without making eye contact, like Cardio is dancing around assiduous waiters.

One woman pulls out a camera and starts to film Cardio from a distance. When he turns and sees her, he freezes with a big warm smile on his face. He cocks his head downward. After draping the monkey on his shoulder, he uses his free hand to lower the glasses farther down his nose and reveal his eyes. One eyebrow rises.

Like he is frozen in a pirouette, he crosses one leg in front of the other. The monkey is back in his hands and he has raised it in the air. "MONKEY! We are in the Future! We are in a camera, being viewed by people in the future! Now is the most amazing now ever!"

He dances for some time, until he grows tired.

42

CHERRY GETS INVOLVED

[2011]

"JIM, this needs more."

"But can't you do it?"

"No. This development, it is more than hours, it is perspectives. Look at this team. One woman and she is just keeping the schedule. Everyone except for me are car-dominant thinkers, some the children of car people. We need more."

Reginald and Cardio had agreed to this in an instant message chat after Reginald had come home from work. The two had found text conversations between them a pleasurable transmutation of their communion. That was a phrase Cardio coined one evening. Sometimes they backlined conversation about Autonomy. Sometimes Cardio asked after Reginald's experience. Reginald got the sense that he was a hot house tomato Cardio had grown, but did not particularly mind. Cardio showed placid caring towards Reginald.

C: **Can SS accomplish this scope?**

R: **Well, not well :>**

C: **What is lacking?**

R: **...**

R: **I have been thinking about this quite a bit. I know we can make a product, but it won't be new enough, aware enough. It will function, but fail.**

C: **What is lacking?**

R: **Damn you.**

They both stared at flashing cursors in their dark apartments.

C: **...**

R: **I know.**

C: **I suspect that you are in a position to bring them (her) into the conversation.**

R: **Damn you, and thank you, and yes.**

Jim was Budget in a meeting. He came in late and the meeting would just restart at the top. Reginald caught him in Jim's office at 8:30 in the morning. Reginald knew that Jim was a morning person and thought faster before 10am.

"SigmaShift has a piece, but this requires triangulation. We are going to produce something myopic. It will fail, no matter how much time or money we spend."

Jim actually looked up at him. He made his Serious Face. "Have you any ideas?"

"Always. My old firm out West. Green Paintbrush."

"Forgot you came from that outfit. Send me a link. Let me think about it."

43

BRADY SMOKING *and* READING

[2011]

IT is a brand new pack of cigarettes, of his favorite brand. Favorite is an unnecessary descriptor. It is his brand. He does have dalliances with an exotic British brand or with the cigarette that he used to smoke years ago. That brand is one of the top two in America and at least a dollar cheaper than the one he smokes today. Back when he sold cars and for the first few years of insurance sales, that dollar mattered.

Now, he smokes whatever brand he wants to. He can't smoke as often as his appetite would like, it is true. Small price to pay for the service he can offer.

He peeks at the window to make sure it is opened. While technically smoke free, the Capital understands that it would be inconvenient for electeds to have to step out. As long as they take care to ventilate properly, no one makes a fuss.

"Oh."

"I figured you would not care. That you would understand."

"Yes, I do, but surprised that you knew that, Senator."

Cardio has been ushered into the room to find Senator Carson leaning towards a cracked window, blowing smoke from a less than graceful stance.

"My name is Cardio Plathemy," he extended his hand and walked towards the Senator. "I am here to talk about some important changes in transportation."

Brady stayed at his position, shifted his cigarette to his left hand and extended his right to meet Cardio's. His left hand moved the cigarette across his body to be near the opened window. "Cars that drive themselves."

"Automotive deaths and injuries plummeting from their unacceptably high levels."

"Robots in control of our safety."

"The end of traffic jams."

"Big brother driving us around."

"The end of traffic jams. Billions of barrels of oil saved. Pollution reduced without the loss of productivity."

"Sure. Pleased to meet you."

"An honor."

"...again, Mr. Plathemy."

"I don't know that we have had the pleasure before, Senator."

"I was not a Senator. I was a car salesman in a Salt Lake City BMW dealership."

Cardio's eyes calculate for three seconds or so. His memory is faultless, but there is sometimes a slight latency. "Interesting, sir. I do recall. Have you another cigarette?"

"Reading today, I realized that you actually had a great effect on my life that year, 1983/84. You were actually at that dealership not to buy a car but to research car culture. I was a horrible car salesman and through lucky chance landed a job after that at the second largest insurance provider in America. I was one of the top salesman in my region following the plan that you laid out for that company to take advantage of Clear and Sane."

Brady reaches into first the left pocket and then the right to find his cigarettes, using his left hand for both. Then he reaches back into his left to retrieve his lighter with the hand that is already holding the cigarette pack. He hands both to Cardio.

"Your information was invaluable. I suspect that the acuity you showed that day is part of why you are here today."

"If I was smart I would not be foolish enough to get elected to the US Senate." They both laugh. "Stay close to the window, please."

Cardio shades the cigarette tip as if there was a wind and flicks the disposable lighter. He had actually brought his own cigarettes but felt that bumming a cigarette from a senator would be an interesting experience. He notes the brand as he hands back the pack and lighter.

Cardio steps towards the window. They are oddly close together as they both considerately blow their smoke out the window. Picture two eighteen-year-olds in a dorm room.

"And now, Autonomy," says Brady.

"Yes, Autonomy. What do you think of the name?"

"Well, it is nothing but positive. Perhaps a little too positive."

"mmm."

"It is fucked up, Cardio, but you are not saying that we the people will be autonomous. You are saying that the machines will be."

A different tone of "mmm" and a drag on a cigarette.

"I would say that Autonomy, particularly capitalized like that, is creepy. Like the geek drool parties over The Singularity." Brady capitalizes with his vocal tones.

"But if you had a choice, would you not want to be the one who had a car with Autonomy versus not having it? It is a feature," said Cardio.

"mmmm."

They smoked, both looking out the window.

"I have always remembered how those essays for the insurance company affected people. I am interested to see where you take us this time, Cardio. I am also curious what you are looking for today. What is your ask?"

Cardio rolled the cigarette back and forth by swishing the second knuckles of his index and second finger together. It was a habit of his, when he smoked.

"I wanted to know what you knew of Autonomy, Senator. You suggest that you know a great deal. I want to know your concerns and what you believe are the concerns of your constituency. Can you speak to that?"

"I know a little bit less than you about what cars and driving mean to my constituency. I think we have similar conclusions, though."

"What might those conclusions be?"

"As I said, I probably know a little less than you. Why don't you tell me what they think?"

While taking another drag, Cardio considers sticking to the script.

"They are unaware of the possibility of change, Senator Carson. Autonomy would be like saying that we never need to pay taxes again. It is a problem that people don't even consider a problem. The issues with driving are a given."

"mmm."

"Conversely, we are asking them to surrender experiences and rights that are 'worth fighting for.'" Cardio does not raise his hands to simulate quotation marks. He does it with his eyebrows and vocal tone, "Freedom. Self determination. Privacy."

"The innovation of the individual. Do you understand the mythic element we are speaking of?"

"I am not sure if I yet understand it. I am still working that. Right now there are two possibilities. One: aspiration. That as Americans lose self-determination in any form they lose their innovative thinking. That the difference between here and Europe and Asia is that we want the risk and experience of driving our own cars."

"mmmm."

"Two: existentialism. That oppression must be battled in all its forms, regardless of the goal of that oppression. It is both of these, but I am not sure which one to defeat in order to win. However, I will tell you our 'trump card.'" Cardio deployed more eyebrow quotation marks.

"Safety." Brady turns toward the window with confidence. There is an odd tray on the outside ledge. He reaches his hand out and stubs the end of his finished cigarette into the tray.

"Very good. Just like Clear and Sane."

"I am not your student. I am your target, your mark."

"More true is that I am your student. Which do you think is more important? Self determination or existentialism?"

"I have no accountability. I can say anything. You are being polite." Brady steps out of the way so that Cardio can thread his arm out the window and extinguish his cigarette.

"You had no accountability at that BMW dealership and you were invaluable to me then. Your insight can only be better now, here in this office."

"This is fascinating, but I have another meeting very soon. A pleasure, Cardio. Please keep my office informed of your efforts."

44

CHERRY FLIES OUT

[2011]

SHE has lost the weight, and looks pretty good. The male attendant whose momentary job is to muster handsome and greet the oncoming passengers shows a not-as-gay-as-I-look interest. She notes it, that her now carefully tinted hair has affected the amount of interest she generates. Her hair as it grows from her head is a dirty blonde. An inconsistent blonde. Now, an enthusiastic Spokane hair stylist crafts a consistent blonde that is equal to a blockbuster film star, touched up in post-production.

Most of her male co-workers did not notice the way they started to refocus their attention on her. She did and felt a little sorry for them, but understood.

Everybody wants some heaven. Everybody wants every day more heavenly. It is a simple early precept. The ultimate original design cue.

It looks brutal, staring down a trans-coastal itinerary from minor airport to minor airport. It will be nearly 12 hours and it will be three planes (changing at two stops) and it will be three hours of jet lag.

She stows the small bright green rolling carry-on above then slides into the window seat. She could think this is brutal or she could be right here for the moment. She does a little of the latter, then settles in to the former.

Her seatmate smiles from the aisle then looks up to the baggage stowage. She breathes in deeply then hoists her soft bag up. A couple two-handed shoves and it seems to fit into the proper space. She sits down, another smile of non-verbal greeting. She is a woman of vague shape.

Large but barely present at all. She wears a soft, linty sweater and over-large pull tie pants. Cherry finds it challenging to picture what this woman's body would be like uncontained by clothing.

They will not talk until the seatbelt sign comes back on for descent. This is normal for the socially fearful normative air traveler. Cherry has found that she is called upon to fly to client face-to-face moments more frequently. She makes a study of the airport world. It is a better experience than being uncomfortable and splayed so far from one's expectations of normal and just.

Cherry falls asleep shortly after takeoff.

Coming in to San Francisco shortly after, there is a ding followed by the handsome attendant's voice reciting a subtle variation on "the captain has turned on the seatbelts sign in preparation for our..." Cherry notices that a young woman, probably fourteen and wearing a hat from a previous era, is actually listening intently to every word of the announcement. It is possible that this is the first time she has ever heard the message and needs to listen to ascertain significance. Cherry pulls out her phone and taps a quick note to think on new travelers' experience. What is it that they feel?

(Perhaps this world is built for them. The architecture of airports, the modes of communication, they are the reason that airports function the way that they do. All of the regulars are at the ready to play a part in the experience of a new audience. Their experience is the same here as at an amusement park. Each turn is a new wonder but they are aware it is highly managed. There are dangers, but all well marked. She can choose her dangers. She can defy the seat belt sign. She can talk to strangers. Ultimately the outcome is set. She will arrive at her aunt's house, perhaps with a story to tell.)

San Francisco. Cherry checks her watch. They are slightly early and the two gates are a short distance apart. Good. Easy. She won't sleep the whole way to Newark and can have some time to get her thoughts together on Autonomy and also on Reginald.

Cherry did not think twice about the assignment. It was a request by Cardio and she had not thought about Reginald for many a moon anyway. This was a most interesting opportunity and there was no strenuous psychosis to be had to keep her away. She is not the kind of person to look for such a thing. Reginald may be, but she can handle that.

SFO always seems like a madhouse at first. You land by watching water rise up to meet the plane then miraculously end up safe on dry land. Then the gangway opens up to a cul de sac that seems like Noah's Ark if Noah was tasked with bringing two of every kind of crazy along until the flood subsides. It is dogs in strollers, metalheads with unlit cigarettes, business men tawdry and emphatically phoning someone.

If you take a step back and take a breath you can see that the space imposes order on them all. They can feel crazy and they can act crazy. But they cannot disrupt their neighbors. Every swipe of a hand is purpose driven. Explicable. Designed, in that ideal of design that feels

Natural

Normal

Inevitable.

The airport has gone from revisions to mere refinements now. The slight variations from O'Hare to Reagan International are perhaps more visible because of the similarity of all the other elements. Large reader boards at major pedestrian exchanges. Changes in floor surface denote food and sitting areas. Advertising that clues you in to which airport you are currently in. The fact that one has proprietary two sided shuttles that mesh with the wall of one terminal, de-couple and then drive straight into the wall of the further terminal is notable because all the other elements are so similar.

Cherry thinks she should get a coffee before her next flight. She sees that her next gate is five numbers away from her current one. There is definitely a gourmet coffee stand within two gates either side. As though the flight attendant had advised her to check if the closest emergency exit is behind her, she looks the opposite direction first to see if the coffee stand is the other direction. It is. She buys a 12 ounce latte.

Cherry never takes the flat escalators. She thinks they are something of a failure of design. The time and energy savings of a traveler are both minimal. They are tempting playthings for children. They experience the maintenance and failures of any long-running machine. Worse, they create an expectation of convenience, of the expectation that this place will not expect any further exertion from you.

Perhaps that is the architectural purpose of them. These are symbols that you don't need to have agency here. Signage, rules, staff, and machinery here will deliver you appropriately. You can turn off. Stop complaining. We are in control of your speed and direction and destination.

Cherry sometimes forgets a drink while it is in her hand or on her desk. She must remember that she got the caffeine as much as the taste. Drink it.

Dear Reginald and Cherry (both of whom will receive a copy of this letter)

By now Cherry's flights should be handled and our accommodations for the first three days booked. Reginald of course will be fine in his own home for that time.

After that we three will be on the open road, residing in a closed system. I have accomplished much in my life but this journey is important. It could leave behind something that I would consider greater than all the other works of my life.

Please bring the best of yourselves along for this ride.

45

THEY TRAVEL *for* SOME TIME

[2011]

COLD is the background of everything. Cherry likes to be reminded of that, so if she feels chilled she does not reach too quickly for a sweater. She likes to feel the prickle of her arms asking for the comfort of clothing. She can think about what comfort is. Comfort sets itself as the opposite of dying, but it is the opposite of suffering, the opposite of life. People allow discomfort to become fear. They fight and sacrifice to preserve the comfort of themselves and of those they love.

Cherry is in the backseat of the car, slightly cold. Cold enough that her arms are prickly. Reginald is at the wheel. He is smoking one of Cardio's cigarettes. The smoke is pouring into the back seat. It is uncomfortable back here.

Cardio is in the passenger seat. He is dressed perfectly for the weather in a light twill jacket, buttoned with large loops and well finished sections of wood. The rustic appearance is genuine to him. Plus, they are easy to undo.

It is early in the morning. In this moment, it is easy enough to fasten the next two up as the weather from the driver's window makes it his way.

There is about four more minutes of Reginald's cigarette yet to burn. A display of the map on the dashboard shows a blue line heading forward from an image of the car and a green line marking where they have been. Cardio knows that Reginald thought long about those colors and the result is ideal for the experience of someone in his seat. He leans against the door so that he can somewhat face Reginald.

This boy. This boy is such a mute.

Reginald is at the wheel. He occasionally touches it, as if a thought orders him to. Other than that he attends to smoking.

It is early in the morning.

Cherry considers asking a question, something that has not quite come to her yet, or it was just there in her mind. It is a really worthy question that would indicate the sunlight breaking up the blue this moment. It would unite with the sunlight and break through Reginald and perhaps even Cardio, that they may be free.

She is uncomfortable, at rest, the cab of the car is without voice right now, it is just smoke and chill coming through the window. They will proceed without the question and no matter. No question would put the brakes on all this.

A car will finally destroy what we think of America, it is clear. It will be warm, easy, and final. The walls between us and that weight of actual America will fall and they will come pouring in, we will come spinning down. What will be left will be colder, she expects.

46

CLEAR *and* SANE, SOME YEARS LATER

[2011, LOOKING BACK]

HE tried, Cardio tried to quantify what Clear and Sane did to America. He has a sense, a whiff, of it. He doesn't really know, because he can't see the opposite stream, the path with no Clear and Sane ruling. With another 30 years of speed inequity.

He has a sense that vehicle design changed, but he does not quite understand that not only did muscle cars disappear, but cars actually suited for an American road were created for the first time. Had he not found the way to get the mental health lobby to work for Clear and Sane, the world would have indeed been a little crazier.

There is no way to measure exactly how crazy, but imagine.

Through debt, it is perfectly normal for someone to pay more than they earn in a year for a vehicle that is engineered for a race track they will never drive. They use their debt car to either speed beyond their ability to drive or to creep forward in traffic that they have no control over. Their sense of ability, of womanhood and manhood, is challenged both if they drive too slow or if they drive too fast.

They rack up debt managing a device that makes them sad every time they get inside.

Sure, Clear and Sane went over budget on the federal side. Some more freewheeling states enforced it irregularly until the 5-4 Supreme Court decision. There were ugly moments.

Ten years later, an academic did a study of studies in which he was granted access to internal research by all the major insurance companies. The overall estimate was that 15,000 fewer Americans died every year because of Clear and Sane. Its a far better way to preserve life than to end overseas wars or require helmets for young bicyclists.

So, Cardio – along with Carl and Don – saved lives and treasure. They succeeded. They made driving a clearer certainty.

47

CARDIO *as* THEY DRIVE

[2011]

BY now they have crossed most of the Southern states. They are cutting north from Sweetwater, Texas towards Oklahoma. At Colorado they will once again bear west. For now it is a wide-open world, night passing. They are comfortable with their roles and processes, these three. The communication is smooth and without confusion.

"Stormy looking clouds up there." Cherry leans to the side and points up. She is in the passenger seat. Reginald is in the back. Cardio sits in the pilot's seat though he is not touching any controls. Three displays glow up on to his face. Cherry has already recorded in her notes that the passenger experience is isolated by the lighting and the focus of some displays on the front left seat. The team will recommend more egalitarian displays.

"I am feeling confident enough in the device that I would sleep in the cockpit, for what that is worth," said Reginald. When he sits in the back he tends to push his head in between the front seats, swishing his attention between the two up front to catch their facial expressions. When in the front seat, he had no need to attend to the person in the back but focused on the driver. Cherry noted all this, not in her formal findings but in her own permanent record of the experience.

"Of course you do," said Cardio from the cockpit. He turned in his seat. The design allowed for the pilot seat to be partially spun towards the other users. This team approved, however deferred to legal and QA to the safety and liability issues. Usability quality was high.

“Of course you would sleep here. You seek that slump. Total security. This vehicle, on these controlled roads, will offer you a very high probability of certainty. The population will demand rigorous safety assurance, far beyond act of god or standard malefactors. This system will be extremely difficult to hack, will be coded for all sorts of issues.

“It is not enough. It will need good winds and fortunate tides as well.

“The whole effort could be stopped by bad coincidence. If there is one poorly timed deer collision or strange incident far out of the statistical norm, particularly if a baby or a precocious child is killed, our system will never be adopted. To the scrap heap. I don’t know if anyone could buy the PR needed to overcome that narrative.

“Never mind the savings in lives and gas and time. Pressure politics prefers the status quo. Our vast, soft culture will prefer waste and death to a new idea. This is a delicate operation. Harder than when I did it in the 80s. We are softer, and so change is harder.”

Cardio lit a cigarette. He has insisted on smoking in the car. He had not spoke like this yet in the trip. He had been his usual business self, some slight jokes just like one would proffer in a long business meeting to break up the time and help people to refocus. Cherry watches him, watches carefully his motions right now. He moves his left hand to the center of the car. Smoke seeps up from his cigarette and touches the ceiling of their cell. Cherry thinks, “Something in his facial expression, perhaps a tension around the nose.”

Cardio exhales smoke directly to the center of the car. “The soft sink, eventually. Never bet on them, no matter how beautiful or logical. The Picts and the Vandals, the Visigoths, the hedge fund managers come in. They have developed a high pain tolerance, perhaps from a family that has become accustomed to pain and deprivation over generations. They have low expectations of physical comfort.”

Cardio taps the cigarette towards the window, but some ash hits the glass and rebounds into the car.

“Cheer for what you believe in but bet the numbers. The numbers for brutality are good. The probability of thriving for those who will call out that death is an option, that total destruction is possible. They bring guns to a knife fight because it is the right thing to do.

"Don't be afraid. That just shows you are ignorant. Death and obliteration are always on the table. A comet could do the job any day. The hungry populations have seen it happen. They have barely escaped. Don't be surprised when they point at obliteration. The room will tilt. If you blink or even shift your weight, you will be lost.

"So, think about your own death every day. Think about everything you make, everything you rely upon as subject to the whim of someone who hates you. Not just hates you, but hates you merely because you stand between her and survival."

Cherry recognizes his lecture voice.

"No one population has ever been soft as us, the coastal Americans just after 2000. We are assured of wins. Losses are not death, not obliteration, not being lost to memory. Our losses are delays of pleasure.

"We have much to fear. From outside yes, but I don't worry for invasion, at least not until our global financial status has degraded further. The concern is from within the nation. Our Picts and Visigoths are right here where we drive today. Those we have kept poor and uninformed. The butt of our jokes.

"The middle of our country is a cockfight battle royale. We are selecting for a pack of the hungriest, the most efficient, the most reckless. They will come at us. And that is just the white ones. The black and Hispanic, they thrive in what you would think of as intolerable conditions. You would sue someone if you lived like them, but they don't sue. They listen and learn. They absorb pain and survive. They see that pain passes, that discomfort and indignity pass. The threat of a bad minute or a bad year need not dissuade them. You two like to learn, but you are not learning this.

"When enough of them figure out how hopeless the status quo is, they will come at us. Be it organized or impulsive, I don't know. I imagine a combination. They will degrade us.

"It is beautiful right now, from a historical perspective. Reginald, when you fuck up, the depth you fall is so very short. One innocent dead, a little unwanted sex. You skip to the next chapter.

"You can recapture any loss you experience very quickly. We don't expect real suffering or risk. We don't game for obliteration, even us three. These might be some of the best minds in America in this car, the best at assessing value and maximizing results. With beautiful design, we reduce risk.

But what are the risks we call out? Slight, very slight possibility of injury. Fiscal loss or reduced profit."

He takes a drag from his declining cigarette. The road curves over his shoulder and the car follows, "It is never obliteration."

Cardio turns back to the front. He motions with his cigarette stump towards the road ahead, "Here, we are allowing this vehicle to take our agency away for the sake of convenience and efficiency. For safety. For social good. No matter. This vehicle is not programmed for hordes of black and Hispanic nor for armed white militias. I am not sure how to program it for that circumstance. I hope that I can fashion something in the next few days. Your ideas are welcome."

"Cherry and Reginald, I want you to know two things." Cardio turns again and raises his pinkie. "I am sorry. I no longer practice any self-control. I personally don't have to. I can do or say anything that I want. It is, I must be honest, a great relief."

Cardio raises his ring finger. "Second, I know enough that I believe enough. I have beliefs built upon so many years of confirmation. I can be fearless like a Vandal, without concern about obliteration. Why? Well, I am not afraid for me. I have fed the dominant culture for a career spanning 4 decades. Now I have no expectation of the traditional idea of legacy.

"I hold legacy in one hand," Cardio lifts his right, cupped hand.

"I hold dust of wherever I stand in the other," Cardio lifts his left hand, also cupped.

"I choose the dust."

Cherry impulsively cups Cardio's chin in her hand. Reginald cranes his neck in all directions. The car sizzles along. Reginald and Cherry are silently trying to fashion the solution they believe Cardio needs, to prepare the system for the inevitable attack.

In five kilometers, Cherry will stop trying to solve that problem. She will turn to the passenger window, the bushes and slight evidence of humanity that pass by and disappear. What we call nature, what we call man. She smiles, rolls the window down. The little moving room shudders and blusters. She sticks her arm out into the world.

48

THEY ARRIVE

[2011]

THEY are done. Their car parks at an industrial park, a nautilus of roads wrapped around two-story buildings of such astounding dullness that they barely exist. Their destination is one of these boring buildings.

They are all silent as the car shuts itself off. They don't reach for the doors. A breath. Another breath.

Reginald is in back again, again peering between the two others. He looks up through the windshield at the flat boring building. Two men and a woman in business attire have come striding through the door. You can make out security IDs on lanyards around all three necks.

"People need enemies," said Reginald. Cardio nods. Reginald continues, "Someone, something unacceptable that eventually, inevitably experiences retribution. They want it so bad."

"People need heroes," says Cherry and she sighs, "who stand for a better version of us, who point at that retribution. We call it justice. Such a pretty word. It helps one stand tall."

The three characters are approaching. Now Cardio can make out their big smiles, even with his aging eyes. "People need endings, but they will never get them."

49

REGINALD *and* MARY

[2010]

MARY and her wheelchair had become one. The seat was cracked in two and swallowed her, butt first.

Her back was contorted around one arm rest. As she shifted she could feel one rib on each side of the padding.

This was not good, not good, not good. Grisly. Mary clasped and unclasped one set of fingers. That wrist was broken, pointing oddly down the road, at the tail lights she could still see.

Grisly. Too drunk to feel it as pain. Per se. Drunk or shock. Pretty drunk, though. Pretty pretty drunk.

Tail lights. Now brake lights. She turns her head and it flops heavily. Something is definitely wrong. Definitely wrong. Definitely.

Her head rolled more. There was a chicken, standing tall in the darkness. Definitely.

He couldn't connect the thump to what he saw. The thump was an ordinary sound of two masses meeting. It was a mundane sound, further muffled by the cab of the truck.

What he saw was unexpected. A wheelchair, traveling backward, motivated by the feet of the rider. Unexpectedly fast, making use of the downhill slope. Where would an itinerant wheelchair racer be heading in the pre-dawn?

This is an hour for restless travelers to get on the road. He had been staring at the strangely speckled motel ceiling through the black. It twisted and changed before him. The wall was doing the same trick. Nothing said sleep. Nothing answered unasked questions.

The first thump was the wheelchair getting partially caught under the front driver side wheel. It then spun bizarrely out in front of the hood, turned and dove under the right hand passenger side wheel. It reappeared on the right, a wholly different thing. This was transformed to an amalgam of hobo and train car. The object was tipped on one side, spinning like a turntable. Reginald figured that it was pivoting on the wheel on the ground. The human head was at completely the wrong angle.

Reginald completed the left turn he had been making. His foot went down onto the gas pedal. Then for a second, the brake pedal. He breathed. He looked up into the side view mirror. The form was not moving. The face was pointed down.

Gas pedal again. Blocks of the city passed by. Now it was worse. Hit and run. Leaving the scene. He is not a pro at physiology, but he thinks it would have been hard to survive.

He does know a lot about perception and he knows that a recipient of those blows would be unlikely to get a license plate number or any reliable information for that matter.

"A large vehicle, maybe, like perhaps a truck or a van. Maybe. White, I think. Not sure."

He is now a couple kilometers away. The freeway onramp appears.

50

MARY PERFORMS DELILAH

[2003]

MARY steps on to the stage. There is a moment that she feels terrified then a moment that she feels completely blank, then a moment that she is breathing in for the first note, where she is putting a finger to the strings of her guitar and she knows how this is going to go.

It is a battered, honored venue, one that probably looks completely derelict in the light of day. In the glistening major motion picture-like contrast of poor house lights under the haze of committed cigarette smoke, switching states in the medley of powerful stage lights, the features of the building are unreal, a place for heroic moments, for historic strides.

And the wires leading out from her guitar goes to a place that makes beauty for her. It is not something she understands but she will sometimes get a shiver for the beauty she can make when she is plugged into her rig and her amp is mic'ed up to a good house system. Sometimes that shiver comes right here, before the first note.

She is on the West Coast, close to home but that doesn't matter. Just back on the road from visiting her friend Lorilee in Montana but that doesn't matter. She is about to play that first chord. It comes with the first words.

"Matter, what's the matter?"

And a bass line flounces on, it lets her ride about it. She sways with the figure of it.

She would sing with her eyes closed if audiences weren't so interesting. The as-one as-many being she is making as she plays on. The characteristic limbs, the finite number of ways one can move on the floor of a contemporary American club. She likes to watch them, improvising what is to her always familiar.

For this tour, she is playing the album completely through, then going back and playing older songs and covers for a second set. The band is getting tighter each night. She is delighted that the result is not rigidity but the ability to be playful and stretch each other without breaking. They keep surprising her, surprising each other. They make jokes with fills, they hail each other well met across the stage with a slight push.

They don't miss much, these three.

These shows, in the mid-sized cities, are starting to sell out. Pitchfork broke quite a champagne bottle over the album upon its release. "The Real Mary Has Finally Arrived" was the headline.

Their interpretation of Delilah was distinctly offset from Mary's own intent. She agonized for a brief while. Thane understood, and said that all the new listeners would surely take their own interpretation, that the truth of Delilah will still be in the songs. She knew he was counting the money to himself. She appreciated that. It was important that someone does.

The first song ends on a trill. The band knows that they can't change the trill. There are signature pieces of the album that have already come up as pennants that the crowd looks to. They have to be there.

In "A New Weight" the drummer holds himself to tom quarter notes for those four measures before the last chorus. The bass player deadens his strings, and he and the keyboard player look down to their feet.

Mary looks over the audience heads. Her lips go flat. She knows it is good. She knows they know what is coming. She knows it is going to be good. The chorus breaks them all into light, into a smile, all their minds break into a flat sprint across a grassy hill, just feeling frisky and grateful to be back on the firm musical surface that Mary constructed for them.

It looks like there will be a second round of bookings, some better venues and a few cities added where sales are picking up. Thane does a good job, she thinks, of avoiding empty dates. Her presence somewhere moves record sales, then record sales bring her back again, which moves more record sales. It makes sense.

The automatic encore is a figure for popular music performances, a choreography between the audience and the musicians. It is absolutely requisite today. To enjoy the experience, either as an audience member or a musician, relax the memory that the encore was once a spontaneous, unusual experience, that it was to note a performance that went above and beyond all expectations. Think to the perverse power that the audience gets to feel, that they are drawing the unwilling musician back to the stage, that they are in control for a moment.

Typically for this tour her encore has been a two-phase cover: she plays Tammy Wynette "Stand By Your Man" as a soulful solo song then transitions it into a raucous, jamming "Gentle On My Mind" with the full band. Glen Campbell's roaming lover calls back to his woman from the road, says thanks, and heads farther afield.

She notes the fading of the last note, and then she turns to go. The Mary that walks off the stage is different. She goes blank for a second and then thinks whether she is hungry, whether she is horny, whether she wants a drink. She is always all of these, every show.

This book wants you to
talk about it. Share online
or casually drop quotes
in conversation.

AFTERWORD

TO CLEAR AND SANE

THE truth of the matter is I started to write this book to make real for me three poets of the modernist era that strike me well and hard.

In college, I read *Three on the Tower* by Louis Simpson. His book was published the year of my birth, 1975. It contextualized and humanized authors that were by my time giants of the English language poetry canon: Ezra Pound, T.S. Eliot, and William Carlos Williams.

I digested Simpson's triumvirate. Williams, the homebody that thrived taking life as it is. Eliot, the talent that breaks, takes, and makes. Pound, the biggest personality, the go-to, the conductor.

These three descriptions are not enough to understand these authors. Don't stop here. Don't settle for a summary. Read them a little, then read Simpson's book.

If writing a book is just covering ground, then I covered the same ground with this novel as I recall Simpson covering in *Three on the Tower.*

I did it because all I wanted (and still want) is to write poetry and be worshiped for that. Those three seemed to have succeeded. In reading *Three on the Tower*, I could see that they are also just people who lived at a time and place. I wanted to be them but they are no different than me. That seemed an interesting tail for me to chase.

In their place and time, they made works that grace lives. They marked up the shared world with useful annotation in a codec that does all our split selves some service.

Here is a wild claim that I cannot substantiate but I believe; You may not read poetry, but the effects of the modernists ripple in your life.

Based on the fame these three achieved compared with a poet today, poetry as the recognized craft for world-annotation has receded. Where do poetry minds go that want to leave a big crater? In the eras where poetry is un-powerful, do the poetic talents look to other industry?

Perhaps in the transformative industrial-to-information age they would work the interfaces and systems being built to surround us.

So my versions of three on the tower are designers of our commercial systems. They think about how to check people into airplanes. They make insurance applications better. They think about how we use our cars and why.

Of the three, Eliot is my dearest. For Williams I have a yearning fascination. I try to grasp Pound but he fades away. My poet friend Frank Sauce surrounds and dives into Pound. Pound is a lodestar for Frank, but I have not managed to finish *The Cantos*. I have read William's Paterson numerous times. The Wasteland and Ash Wednesday I have read beyond counting.

H.D. I developed late for this book, in a burgeoning realization of my sexist filter. The characters asked me what would happen if the contemporary avatars for modernist poetry actually made art instead of ATM interfaces, so she worked that question for us.

The characters have no past. I started to write biographical origin stories, but it was clear I was going to reverse engineer lives and frames from my own fallacies. It is a practice of contemporary writing – for some the whole reason for writing. It didn't work here.

My attempts quickly looked like Freudian justifications. I decided that recalling your childhood halfway through a book is a device few can do without dehumanizing the character. That it takes the mind of the reader out of their hearts and devolves them into readers of a story. I avoided their pasts so these characters and their readers could meet in the moments they encounter each other. Williams got a short shot to make a point that none of them cared where they came from.

How modernist of me.

I don't know that I intended to cloak the inspirations for these characters as much as Clear and Sane ultimately does. What I knew – believed – of Eliot, Pound, H.D., and Williams guided the hands of these characters until the writing magic occurred and the characters took over.

I did not have a plot in mind. Reginald, Mary, Cherry, and Cardio found the storyline.

Most interesting to me in the process of writing was my own allegiances. The poet that I could never grasp turned into the soul engine of my own novel. I had figured that my dear troubled friend would be the ingenue but instead he descended.

So there are the Modernists standing on the bridge, pleading to free us from autobiography. Pointing to the world as it is right now, urgent that our hearts could rise up through math, finance, petty psychology, imposed shame-built morals, and the heft of single-generation tradition.

And here they are poets not making poetry because there is no power in it these days.

And yes, you will hear again of the surviving characters. We have more poetry to speak.

ACKNOWLEDGMENTS

TEN years of haze has passed since I wrote the bulk of the drafts for this book. I am grateful I have the text to remind me. These last few months of wrangling that string of words into a book, however, are strong in my memory.

I decided to skip the publishing houses and publish myself, using some of the more beneficial aspects of our era's tech. That means looking to my family and community for their skills and support. I needed this string of words to have a beautiful launch into the world and into your hands. That would not have been possible working alone.

Those who joined the Kickstarter to fund this project not only made it possible financially, they showed me that I was worth this attention. I am so grateful, in particular for the generosity of

Beloved Sarah Ratay
Brother Patrick Johnson
Cousin Arlo Miller and his generous other-cousin Ilana Goldstein
Brethren Leo Marcel Schuman

I have to also thank Leo for building Old Truck Good Coffee (**oldtruckgoodcoffee.com**) with me, where we both have forged confidence, tightened our writing, and grew in our understanding. Leo is a helluva compatriot to have.

I would never have become the person that could complete this project without the people that held me in crisis and idiocy, with the grace of community and family. To list them all is risky for the possibility that I would forget someone. Thanks to all that brought me here.

Thank you to the early readers who I had to ask "is this a novel?" Matt Flaming and Danielle Frandina. They were nice enough to insinuate "it is not a book...yet."

Gabe Trout who patiently enabled the web infrastructure for **joelbyronbarker.com** and **thegreenpaintbrush.com**. I managed to break DNS setting each one up. He fixed the Internet both times for me. Didn't even give me a tsk tsk.

David Stewart, who helped work through digital frustrations with me to make sure The Green Paintbrush has a proper digital presence.

The beautiful book you hold in your hand (even the ebook version) was made real by Lisa Dorn, as was all the good-looking marketing materials. Lisa is an adept designer who uses her empathy and curiosity to make projects match the spot in the world they belong. I wager she is blushing while typesetting this. Seek her out at lisadorndesign.com.

My father Lee Barker was the last editor of this string of words and the first to show me the pleasure of stringing words together. He is to this day a gentle editor of my life, providing markup and attaboys. Thank you for this shared love of the intricate details of language and of big awkward projects.

My mother Diana Barker is all over this book, sharing the question "what do we do next?" with myself and these characters. She is a guide to me in how to live well by imagining the possible into reality.

Aunt Cathy who lives the way she wants to – as generously as possible – inspiring me to do the same.

And to Sara Quinn Thompson, constantly generous with her time and input and love. The idea to bring The Green Paintbrush out into our world was hers. All this work and risk feels easy when I talk to you, Sara. Let's keep talking.

Let's all keep talking. My last acknowledgment is you, who has opened this book. When you read this, we are creating together. I thank you for creating with me.

Joel Barker
Thereabouts
Autumn 2025

APPENDIX
POETRY

Please note dear reader that none of this section need be bothered with.

DRAFT, 2010, SPOKANE

You start here, where
you are, having thrown everyone away.
Whatever happened before
Is the paper. And now is
The English ink sinking into the continent.
And I am sinking into the continent.
This is how it goes.
The garbage becomes
furniture.
I could believe anything
Here
On the eternal beginning.
The camera has pulled back and almost
Like it belongs,
There is the tank that feeds the rain machine.
An imperfect part of the street is in view.
2 folks, pale
washed out unmade faces,
glance at the camera
then turn away.
But even that is a perfect performance. I will take
It. I am not in the least disappointed. In fact,
I breathe in through pursed lips when I see the

Water tank. You can
Hear me. And I turn to one side and put my index
Finger to my jawbone when the first crew member looks
up. I make a fist with that hand when he looks down.
My motions are almost theatrical,
Eh. Posed poetics. A faux
Moment, illustrative of only
Worthwhile tension – that this is developing indeed.
I carry on. It is how things develop. Sometimes, other
Days. Stillness.
I carry on. It is how things develop. Sometimes. Other
days. Stillness.
It is somewhat organic. If there
Is any machinery, any
System to it, I can
Not devise how to describe it.
I have become better at
the right move for it
at this time or that time.
Then worse again.
I can
Be sure that anyone
Who survives to forty and
Has the ability to dress themselves
For dinner can somewhat conceive what I mean.
I assume that there are
so many awful, stupid and
still-minded people in the
world. I forget as I have become

rather good at avoiding them –
and repelling them.
Antiquarian language,
Such-is-this statements and
Being boring in an entirely
Uninviting way does the trick.
That if I encounter then at all.
My territories are not often
Their habit anymore.

Posthumously Released, written circa 2022

It's shorter than a lot of his more known work, and was meant for a private audience, not released to the world until long after his death, due to some private concerns specified in his estate. All completely unfounded:

At a loss
Beautiful, though tripped up and a bit ripped up
Either ascending or descending. Hard
To discern and it doesn't matter
One slight rip in the stocking, just a
Spot of skin.
Somehow also a faucet.

www.ingramcontent.com/pod-product-compliance
Lightning Source LLC
Chambersburg PA
CBHW060545310726
48982CB00009B/1381/J

* 9 7 9 8 9 9 3 8 4 6 3 0 9 *